THE *Mystery* OF A LOST SWORD AND SCIMITAR

*A historical novel for young
persons under the age of 91
(and of course, their parents!)*

BETTY BALMFORD

The Mystery of a Lost Sword and Scimitar

Spiderwize
Remus House
Coltsfoot Drive
Woodston
Peterborough
PE2 9BF

www.spiderwize.com

A CIP catalogue record for this book is available from the British Library.

The views expressed in this work are solely those of the author and do not necessarily reflect the views of the publisher, and the publisher hereby disclaims any responsibility for them.

All characters in this publication are fictitious except those who are prominent in history.

ISBN: 978-1-911596-44-8

For Andrew and Georgie

This book is dedicated to my David without whose help and support it would never have been printed. He has dotted every I and crossed all my Ts. He added a thousand verbs! *(I hate verbs!).* He has spent many hours producing the cover and masterminding the graphics, typing my pencil scrawl and preparing the whole manuscript for publishing.   (*There is a verb in that sentence*!).

Also to our sons, Andrew and Timothy, their wives Georgie and Liz, and our friends and family and pets. (*There is no verb in that phrase*!)

With my love.

Mum.

(Betty Balmford)

Damascus, Hattin, Tiberias and
Jerusalem on a modern map.

CONTENTS

The Beginning.. 1

To Guy's House.. 14

Fishing.. 21

Sue and Christopher... 31

The Civil War... 37

The Passages 45

Saturday 55

An Old Box 65

More Tales - The Crusades 72

The Battle of Hattin 85

Guy.. 93

Alive! 105

Young Man for Sale 115

SOLD!.. 126

A Secret Room 137

Thursday 147

Beneath the Stone 153

The Trunk... 163

Into the Chapel... 176

The Finish 182

Bibliography 185

About the Author.. 186

CHAPTER 1

THE BEGINNING

My story begins on an ordinary Thursday in early August, but that Thursday would affect the rest of my life; I didn't know it then of course. It was my birthday next day and my best friend from school, Guy Villiers, was coming to stay on Saturday for a couple of weeks.

I had helped Mum clear the spare room - my junk mostly. My Gran had given us a counterpane that she had crocheted for his bed and I had cleaned the window, well, sort of. The room had never looked so good for ages, just waiting for Guy.

We had planned so much those last days at school - days at the beach - fishing - swimming in the rock pool at Treyarnon - I couldn't wait. Dad had bought a second-hand bike and had replaced the chain, brakes and the gears. I had polished the frame until it looked almost new and now it sat in the shed next to mine, again just waiting for Guy.

The phone rang. With that phone call it seemed that my whole world came crashing about my ears. My Grandpa had had a road accident in France, was unconscious in a small French hospital and Mum had to get herself and Gran to France if possible that evening on the Plymouth to Roscoff ferry. It was decided that I had to go to stay with Aunt Winny in Exeter until my Dad got back from Iran.

Aunt Winny! Oh perish the thought! She was my Dad's aunt and lived in a small house in Exeter with a bad tempered elderly cat who had taken an intense dislike to me. When we had visited in the past, it would hide behind doors and furniture waiting to ambush me and then as I passed, spring, fastening its claws into my arm, leg or even my head, trying to tear me to pieces. (When I think about it even now I shudder). And then a sudden thought struck me. I looked at Mum and said in a very small voice 'What about Guy?' Mum's face fell.

'Oh Luke. I'm so sorry.' She suggested I ring him up and explain, which I did. Then she talked to his Mum.

I went up to Guy's room. It had the best view of the coast and I watched the sea crashing on the rocks in the distance, tide must have been in. I thought of all our plans and his bike in the shed and then of my lovely Grandpa in hospital. I was so miserable.

I heard the phone ring again, probably Aunt Winny. Mum came upstairs calling me. 'Come and help me pack your bag. That was Guy's Mum on the phone. She invited you to go to Guy's house to stay if I can get you to Exeter by 2 to 2.30 this afternoon. They have a friend staying in Exeter who is going home to Oxfordshire on the 3 o'clock train and will take you with her.'

Everything seemed to happen in a mad rush after that. I was so excited and could hardly speak. We packed, picked up my Gran from her cottage and drove like the wind, getting to Exeter before 2 o'clock. We met Mrs Ann Jones, Guy's Mum's friend, at her hotel. Mum and

Gran then set off to Plymouth and Mrs Jones and I went to catch the train to Reading. She told me to call her Ann. I sat by the window watching the world go.

'I wonder how my Grandpa is?' I said. 'He's had a road accident in France.'

'So I understand. Was he on holiday?' asked Ann.

'Yes. He went there every so often, meeting old farmer friends he'd met during the last war.'

'Oh! Was he in France during the war?'

'Yes. He was a pilot photographer.' I replied.

'Goodness! That sounds exciting.'

'It was. He got shot down in France. Would you like to hear about him?'

'Yes. It'll pass the time 'til we reach Reading.' Ann answered.

'Well, ' I said, wondering where to start, trying to remember the story as my Grandpa had told it. I don't remember how well I told it that day sitting in the train to Reading, but as my Grandpa's accident was the beginning of my story anyway, I'll tell it myself now.

He was a lovely man and we were great friends. He was half French and spoke French like a native which was very useful to him as you will see. He had joined the Royal Air Force as a pilot having learned to fly before the war. However, when the RAF discovered he had been an accomplished photographer working for a newspaper, he was immediately posted to the Photographic Reconnaissance Unit (PRU) at St Eval in Cornwall.

He loved flying. 'Can you imagine' he said one day, 'taking off on a cold wet windy day, then climbing up through the thick grey rain clouds and suddenly breaking through - up and up - and finding sunshine and blue sky stretching as far as the eye could see, and below you a carpet of snow white fluffy clouds. One had the whole world to one's self. That was flying.' I later learned that flying for the PRU during WW2 was not all sunshine and blue skies.

The RAF had modified Spitfires into unarmed photographic flying machines. They were equipped with Rolls Royce Griffon engines (later powering the Shackleton), stripped of all unnecessary weight and filled up with extra fuel. They were set up with cameras and film, and everything the photographic pilot would need. Pilots like my Grandpa then flew over Europe taking pictures bringing back vital information about the war and what the enemy was doing. Bomber Command used these pictures when targetting such things as petrol storage dumps, important bridges in fact anything that could hamper the enemy's efforts to invade England.

He flew many lonely nights over Europe but one night disaster had struck. His plane was caught in a German searchlight and was immediately attacked by their anti-aircraft guns. His plane was hit and damaged and he was forced to bail out. The aircraft though damaged, had crash landed in one piece, skidding to a halt, burying its nose in the hedge at the edge of the field.

German patrols had heard the drone of the damaged aircraft as it flew over the countryside and also the distant crash as it hit the ground. However there had been a lot of rain over the past few weeks and the land was very wet and muddy making it impossible to drive any sort of vehicle across the farmland fields. They were obliged to set off on foot with their dogs in the hope of finding survivors.

This situation probably saved my grandfather's life because a group of French farmers had also heard the crash. They had been playing cards in the large cellar of Andre's barn. When France was invaded by the Germans in 1940 these farmers had hidden a vast quantity of wine in the cellar. Since then they had met once a week to play cards, eat cheese and bread and drink the wine, in the safety of the French countryside far away from German patrols.

However, this night was different. A plane had crashed into the field quite close to the farm. They rushed out of the barn into the still night to investigate and set off across the fields. The plane had gouged its way across a field of cabbage and here the Frenchmen found it jammed into the hedge. They scrambled aboard but finding no injured airman they turned their attention to the plane's cockpit. They found Grandpa's leather helmet and goggles. There, too, were the cameras and metal tins of film, vital maps and navigation instruments, a tin of corned beef sandwiches and a large slab of chocolate.

Realising that the Germans must not find any of this highly secret equipment, and having no intention of leaving the sandwiches or the chocolate behind, they set about stripping the cabin of anything that could endanger the pilot should he be caught.

Suddenly one of them said 'Hush!' In the silence they could hear the baying of dogs in the distance, probably bloodhounds, coming towards them with a patrol obviously looking for the plane. They jumped quickly off the plane and divided the equipment and the chocolate between them. They trampled the mud around the plane leaving no recognisable boot prints. They broke the sandwiches into bits and scattered them on the ground around the plane. Then these five wonderful Frenchmen set off in different directions to their own farms leaving a mixture of scents to totally confuse the dogs and the patrol.

When the patrol finally arrived at the plane the poor dogs, instead of finding one good traceable scent of the pilot, found only a confusion of smells and the corned beef sandwiches! The patrol, by the light of their torches, realised that someone had got there before them. It had taken them too long to get to the plane.

Grandfather meanwhile, knowing nothing of this at the time, had landed quite close by in a copse of trees. His parachute had caught the branches of a tall tree and he was left hanging by the straps about 50ft off the ground. The sky was clear and the countryside was very still. 'I heard an owl quite close by. Probably wondering why I was swinging in his tree!' smiled grandfather, whilst he told me the story one evening as we sat by the fire.

'It was a funny situation, Luke.' he said. 'I could hear a dog barking some distance away. I could also hear the baying of hounds and the sound of men's voices carrying across the stillness, probably looking for me. It was quite frightening. I was completely helpless just swinging in a tree. I suppose I was lucky to be alive but worse was yet to come.' Listening to my Grandfather, I remember wondering what could possibly be worse but he continued his story.

'I had twisted my ankle as I scrambled out of the plane. Got it jammed somehow. Well,' he continued 'by now it was very painful and throbbing and my beautiful suede fleece-lined flying boot felt very tight. I thought foolishly that if I could loosen the zip which ran all the way up the front of the boot I could reduce the pressure and the pain. I struggled for ages to lift my boot up high enough to loosen the zip.

'When one is hanging from a set of straps in a tree it's difficult to lean forward. Then, at last, I finally managed it. I bent my knee as far as I could and grabbed the top of my boot with one hand managing to loosen the zip with the other. I let my leg drop - and the boot fell off landing on the ground below me. That of course meant certain capture. No dog worth his salt would miss that boot lying at the foot of the tree and no patrolman worth his salt would neglect to look up and could not fail to see me hanging there. I really thought that was the end of me. I might even be shot as a spy. I would certainly be taken prisoner. But by then I was tired out. My luminous watch told me it was after one o'clock. No point in worrying and I must have fallen asleep.'

'When I awoke it was daylight. The birds were singing and it was just after 6am. My legs felt like lead weights. It was very difficult trying to move. The straps of the parachute held me firm. I was thirsty, cold and very miserable. It was then I heard a sound some way off. I listened. Yes - somebody was out there. Then I heard a dog bark. It was a dog - not a hound. I heard a man's voice calling the dog both getting closer to my tree.'

'The dog came through the trees - a black and white collie. It seemed to be making a beeline for my boot. The man appeared in pursuit of the dog calling its name which sounded like Nim. I think I stopped breathing. The

"We're back!" and then she resumed her
attack on my boot.

animal reached my boot. It snuffled round it and then picked it up. The boot, being quite a big heavy thing, was not easy for the dog to carry. However, the man by now had reached the dog and rescued my precious boot. He took it off the dog turning it over probably wondering who could possible loose ONE boot'

'He looked like a farmer. He wore an old jacket over a pair of overalls and a stout pair of Wellington boots. I decided he would eventually look up and see me. I had two choices - to hang there and hope to somehow get down by myself - or shout for help. I was seriously wondering whether my legs and feet would ever work again and it was a long way down if I fell and I might break something. This fellow would surely help get me down in one piece even if he handed me over to the authorities.'

'So I shouted something like "Hi" or "Hello" or "Yoo-hoo" - I can't remember but the dog immediately looked up and barked. The man too looked up and I shall never forget the look of total surprise on his face. He said something under his breath which I didn't really catch but sounded like "Mon Dieu!" and then he grinned. A big wide friendly grin and said "Good morning, monsieur. Nice of you to drop in." All in French of course.'

'He asked if that was my Spitfire that fell into his field last night. I told him it was. "And are there any more crewmen likely to be hanging around?" And then he chuckled. I explained I was alone. "Very well, monsieur." he said. "Wait there. I'll be back." I thanked him explaining I wasn't planning to go anywhere just then being a bit tied up. He looked up at me and laughed again. He called his dog who was now trying to bury my boot and set off into the woods.'

'After about half an hour I heard voices. They got nearer. I was so afraid; was it a patrol of soldiers? My boot was still at the bottom of the tree. They couldn't fail to see it. They would probably fall over it. Perhaps the friendly farmer had reported his find to the patrols and was guiding them back to arrest me. There was nothing I could do but wait. As I looked down watching, the dog was first to arrive. She stood on her back legs looking up at me whining as much as to say "We're back!" she then resumed her attack on my boot.'

'Five men finally arrived carrying two very long ladders and to my relief, no soldiers. They all looked like farmers.'

'How ever did they get you down?' I asked.

'Well,' he said 'they put both ladders against the tree up behind me and tied them together all the way up. One fellow then climbed up behind and above me until he was way above my head. He was carrying a very large curved knife and I could feel him moving the straps which were my lifeline. I hoped he wasn't cutting them. Two of the men then came up one on each ladder and twisted me around to face the tree. To my surprise I was quite close to the trunk and I was then able to hold the ladders. I explained that I had no feeling in my legs and feet as one chap below placed my feet onto the rungs of the ladder. Then with one man on each side they crossed hands behind my back taking my weight. "Attention!"one of them shouted and I realised that the fellow above was cutting my straps. I was told to hold on tight to the ladder. I needed no telling. The ground was a long way down.'

'My original farmer friend was below me on the ladder supporting my legs and feet. I felt the straps go loose as they were cut through. Slowly, inch by inch, they got me down, the man above holding the straps taking some of my weight, the two at my sides supporting my back, the chap below holding my legs and the fifth fellow holding the ladders. '

'I was never so glad to feel solid ground. They laid me down beneath the tree. The dog jumped all over me and licked my face. I tried to stand but my legs collapsed under me and my ankle was very painful. So they put me on one of the ladders and stretchered me back to Andre's farm. The dog decided to bring my boot. She tried to carry it but it was heavy and got in the way of her front legs. Having fallen over it twice the intelligent animal decided it would be a better idea to turn round and drag it, which she did all the way back to the farm.'

'In the weeks that followed I was hidden in Andre's cellar and cared for by him and his wife. After a few days I was able to walk unaided. Food during the war was very scarce and so all five of my rescuers helped to feed me. Once a week I played cards and drank their wine and ate bread and cheese. We became great friends and we must never forget what brave men they were. If they had been discovered hiding and helping me they would all have been shot, not only them but probably their wives and families too. They all took great risks and I owe them my life.'

'Then one day, Henri, one of the five, came to say I was going home if our luck held out. An escape route had been planned. I was to travel, always at night, across France, into Spain and then on to Gibraltar. Henri and

Andre would take me as far as Bayonne. I would be taken on an organised escape route planned by the French Resistance to get allied aircrew back to England.'

'My five rescuers and I became firm friends and decided that, after the war, we would get together every couple of years to talk about old times, eat plenty of bread and cheese, and drink lots of red wine.' It was on such a trip to France that my Grandfather had his road accident.

Years later Grandfather explained what had happened. He had stepped off the curb at the bottom of a hill. He assured my Grandmother that he had looked to his right before doing so. Unfortunately for him, he'd forgotten that the French drive on the right and so the nearside traffic was coming from his left. He failed to see, and was hit forcibly by, a small Frenchman on a large fast-moving bicycle both doing about 40 miles per hour downhill. The man was an onion seller and the bike was loaded with about 30 kilos of onions on strings. The Frenchman, having spent most of the morning in the local pub drinking huge quantities of red wine, was very drunk.

He had hit Grandpa with such force that he had left his bike and onions in a heap in the gutter with Grandpa. He had continued his journey by air for about three meters (according to an eye witness), landing with such a thump that he dislocated his shoulder and broke four ribs. Grandpa had hit his head on the curb and was out cold for two days.

At a later inquiry, Grandpa explained, the Frenchman was asked by the magistrate how he had managed to hit my Grandfather. He answered 'Very easily, Sir! I had my eyes shut at the time.'

The magistrate went blue in the face and asked 'How could you expect to stop if you couldn't see danger ahead?'

'Oh! I couldn't stop, Sir, even if I'd had my eyes open.' explained the Frenchman

'Why not?' asked the spluttering magistrate?

'The bike, she had no brakes, Sir, and she goes very fast down that hill when she is loaded with onions, so it's best to close my eyes. That way I don't see anything. I've never hit anything yet, Sir, until now that is, but I'm not likely to hit anything else.' he added quietly.

'Thank goodness! But why not?' asked the magistrate.

'Well, yes the bike, Sir, she's a bit bent, Sir. Frame's all twisted and a wheel fell off.'

Grandpa, realising that he was partly to blame for the accident, bought the fellow a new bike with a trolley on the back for his onions.

CHAPTER 2

TO GUY'S HOUSE

I must have fallen asleep because I awoke with Ann shaking my shoulder.

'We're almost there.' she said. 'Reading next stop.'

We collected our cases together as the train slowed down, gliding into the station. I watched the faces of the many people waiting on the platform looking anxiously at the train as we slowly came to a halt. Suddenly a face I recognised! It was Guy looking eagerly at all the windows. I was so excited.

'There's Guy.' I shouted.

'Oh good!' said Ann. 'They said they would meet the train.'

Ann opened the door and I jumped down onto the platform shouting 'Guy!' at the top of my voice. There was a very pretty lady standing beside him with her hand on his shoulder. He saw me and dashed to meet me. She followed him.

'Hello! You must be Luke.' she said, 'We're very sorry to hear about your Grandfather but we're so pleased you're able to come to stay with us.'

Guy was leaping about like a demented rabbit shouting

over the noise of the trains and the bustle of the station. 'Glad you're here. Been waiting ages on this platform. Thought you'd never get here.'

With a little help from Guy and me, we struggled out of the station to their Landrover stowing the luggage in the back. We set off out of the station with Ann and Guy's mother chatting in the front. Guy and I sat behind and I don't think we stopped talking all the way, as we drove through the Oxfordshire countryside. Driving through a pretty village of old thatched-roof cottages the car came to a halt outside one of them. The front door opened and three spaniel dogs rushed out barking and jumping at the gate, closely followed by a man.

'They saw you coming.' he laughed. 'Recognised your car. DOWN BOYS! DOWN.' he yelled at the dogs. 'Let your mistress in.'

'Who's that?' I asked.

'Ann's husband - Tim.' whispered Guy. 'He's a friend of my Dad and Uncle Christopher.'

I shouted over the barking dogs, 'Thank you, Ann.'

'Pleasure!' she grinned. 'Guy, you must bring Luke over one day to see those prehistoric stone tools that Tim collected from around your farm.'

'Tim's an archaeologist.' explained Guy. 'He's just back from Egypt.'

Everybody began shouting 'Bye for now!' and Guy's mother said 'The men are getting together next week sometime, Ann, to sort out a puzzle of Christopher's. Why don't you come with Tim? I'll do supper and we girls can get involved.'

'Love to.' said Ann as we drove off.

'Not long now, Luke,' said Guy's Mum, 'it's been a long day for you.'

'Yes.' I answered thinking of that early phone call from my Gran. 'This morning seems like days ago.'

We drove away through the Oxfordshire countryside for what seemed like ages and then as we were driving past a high red brick wall Mrs Villiers said 'Almost there,Luke. This wall is the edge of our estate. The house is up on the hill.' The car slowed down and turned towards a huge wrought iron gate.

'Home,' said Guy, jumping out of the car. 'Come and give me a hand with the gate, Luke!' He unclipped the catch and we both pushed. It was heavy and squeaked a bit on its big hinges. On the centre of the gate was a large metal plaque the shape of a warrior's shield. Across the center were mounted two crossed weapons.

'That's our family crest.' said Guy looking up at the shield. 'There is a sword and the other thing - that's a scimitar. It's a kind of sword used by the Turks hundreds of years ago. At the time of the Crusades, one of my ancestors, a chap called Guy like me, went on a crusade to the Middle-East. He fought against the Turks and the Saracens and he brought the scimitar back. It was said to be solid gold! Uncle Chris told me all this.'

Guy sounded so clever. I hadn't a clue what he was talking about. Who were the Turks and the Saracens, what were the Crusades and what was a scimitar? I remember nodding - hoping he would think I understood it all, which I didn't, but I promised myself I would find out. Perhaps my Dad would know. We jumped back into the car having closed the gate.

'The crest was designed many years ago, Luke.' said Mrs Villiers. 'There's a Latin inscription around the edge which says "ORIENS ET OCCIDENS PACE SEMPER TRANQUILLI" which means East and West at Peace Forever Still. The weapons you see there represented a large part of a family treasure that was lost or mislaid in 1649 by a Harry de Ville who had fought with the King against Oliver Cromwell.'

'A treasure!' I thought. 'Wow!'

'How did he loose it? He must have been very careless.'

'We don't know.' she said. 'Perhaps he dropped it in the Thames or sold it.' she laughed. 'The family can trace its ancestry back to 1068. There has been a house on this hill since the land was gifted to a Count Guy de Ville by his friend William the Conqueror, for the Count's help conquering England in 1066.'

'Since that time, much of the land has been sold off and we are now left with about 200 acres. There's a farm house and four farm cottages in the valley and the Lodge, over on the hillside.'

'Uncle Christopher and Aunt Sue live there.' said Guy.

'Who is Uncle Christopher?' I asked.

'He's married to my Dad's twin sister - my Aunt Susan. He's a historian and knows all about our family history.'

'But your name is not de - what was that French Count's name?'

'De Ville.' Guy's Mum said. 'No, it's not. When England and our Duke of Wellington were fighting the French in the early 1800s, it was not such a good idea to have a French surname. So about 170 years ago our ancestor living here then, changed the family name to

Villiers and we've been Villiers ever since. Come on now, end of story, it's past supper time.'

We drove up to the house. 'Get Luke's suitcase out of the back and take him up to his bedroom, Guy, while I put the car in the garage.'

We went into a large porch filled with Wellington boots, mackintoshes, fishing nets and rods, then through into a big kitchen, on into the hall and up the stairs.

'These are the back stairs.' said Guy. 'Another staircase goes up from the front of the house.'

The house was on three floors. The bedrooms were right at the top. Guy's was next door to mine. I looked out of the open bedroom window. The evening sun was shining and I could see for miles over the green countryside to the hills in the distance. I could also see the river Thames snaking its way through the fields until it disappeared. 'Where does the river go that way?' I asked Guy pointing to my left.

'London' he answered 'but it's a long way. And that way' he said pointing to the right 'it goes through Reading to Oxford. Come on!' he added 'Let's go down to supper. I'm hungry.'

We ran down to the ground floor and the big kitchen. Guy's mother was setting the table and smiled as we went in. 'Mac has done us sausage and mash.'

'Ooooooh goody!' said Guy.

'Who's Mac?' I asked.

'She's Andrew's wife and Mum's friend. She and Andrew manage the farm. She's always been known as Mac because she used to be Miss Mackenzie.' said Guy. 'She helps Mum and shows visitors around the house.'

'People visit? Do they pay, Mrs. Villiers?'

'I'm afraid they do.' laughed Guy's mother. 'But please call me Liz. The money is needed to help pay for repairs and the roof at the back is leaking. Ah well! We can only do our best and hope the house doesn't fall down or the roof doesn't blow off before we can afford to get it replaced. Parts of the house are very old. Over the years our ancestors have spent their time knocking bits off and building bits on until we have what you see today, quite a big mansion. In the main hall there is a picture of what the original house may have looked like in the 11th and 12th centuries. It was drawn by Andrew and just looks like one of our barns.'

Guy and I went back upstairs after supper. He came into my room and sat on my bed while I unpacked my case. 'Mum and Dad are very worried about the house.' said Guy. 'Some horrid men came to see them. They want to buy the house and all the land for a lot of money but my Dad doesn't want to sell.'

'What do they want the house for?' I asked.

'They want to turn the house into a country manor hotel. They plan to use this house, all the cottages and the lodge for their holiday guests. They're going to turn the farmhouse into an old English pub and have a nine-hole golf course on the land down by the river. They're also planning river trips on big boats up and down the Thames. My Dad says they want to turn the whole place into a very big expensive holiday camp. Mum and Dad are horrified at the thought of it. Dad said we really don't have enough money to keep the house going but he doesn't want to sell it to those awful men.'

His Mum put her head round the door. 'Time you were

asleep. It's after 10 o'clock and you've got two whole weeks to talk. Come on Guy, to bed.'

We all said good night. I snuggled down in the soft comfy bed. The window was still wide open and I could see the sky and hundreds of stars.

CHAPTER 3

FISHING

I opened my eyes and for a moment wondered where I was, and then remembered and - WOW - that wonderful feeling of excitement! I was at Guy's house! The sun was pouring into the room, the windows were wide open and the birds were singing fit to bust. What was more, it was my birthday!

I turned over onto my back and realised that the bedroom door was open a tiny bit and Guy's face was peering at me through the crack.

'Thank goodness,' he said, 'I thought you'd never wake up.'

'What time is it?' I asked.

'Nearly half past seven.' he replied, looking at his watch. 'I've been awake for hours but Mum said I wasn't to wake you. Anyway, get dressed and come down to breakfast.'

'What are we going to do today?' I asked. He was wearing his swimming trunks and I thought 'Thank goodness Mum packed mine.'

'Well,' said Guy 'I thought we might go fishing. Hurry

up and get dressed. Mum is taking us to the village to get some bait after breakfast.'

He left and then came back. 'By the way! Mum said you must put on a shirt or something. It's going to be hot and she doesn't want us sun burnt.'

Breakfast was in their big old kitchen. It had red stone tiles on the floor and a large wooden table. There were wooden beams running overhead across the ceiling with huge hooks screwed into them.

'What a big kitchen!' I said, looking at Liz.

'Yes it is but in the past there would have been lots of servants in here all busy cooking huge meals for the family and their guests. The house is very old as I explained last night. Quite a big wing was added in the time of Queen Elizabeth 1 but they didn't quite join the two walls together. That's how we got our secret passages which run between the two buildings.'

'SECRET PASSAGES!' I almost choked on my toast. 'Really?'

'Oh! Hasn't Guy told you about them?' she grinned. 'You'll have plenty of time to explore the house later but not now. I have to go to the village, prepare your picnic and get you off to the river. I'm catching the 11.40 train to London to see the dentist so I shall see you both for supper. Uncle Chris and Aunt Sue are at home all day so go to them if you need anything. Aunt Sue is doing tea for you about half past four and I should be back by six o'clock with your Dad, Guy. Now eat up and let's get off to the village; I need bread and you boys need fishing bait from Mr. Ford.'

Mr Ford owned the sports shop. He sold bicycles,

tennis rackets. footballs and because the village was so close to the river, everything one needed to fish. So, while Guy's Mum went to the baker's, Guy and I went into the sports shop.

'Hello, Mr Ford.' said Guy. The man grinned.

'You've come for some bait!'

'How did you know?'

'Oh! I'm a Wizard!' He took Guy's tin and disappeared into the back shop.

I wandered over to a rack of fishing rods. I remember thinking how much I would love one of them. Guy came over and we inspected the rack together. I had never seen so many rods all shining and new. Guy selected one and took it out of the stand.

'This one's like mine.' he said.

'Lucky thing.' I answered.

'Here you are.' said Mr Ford holding out the tin of bait. 'And here is the thing your Mum ordered.' He handed Guy a long thin box wrapped in brown paper and tied with string.

'What's this?' asked Guy.

'Ah well, Laddie! You'd perhaps better ask your Mam.'

At that moment, Mrs. Villiers came into the shop. She was carrying a basket of hot fresh-baked bread. Whenever I smell fresh baked bread I remember that day in Mr Ford's shop.

'What must you ask me?' she said grinning at Mr Ford.

'What's in here?' said Guy holding out the parcel.

'I really have no idea! I haven't seen inside the box.'

She laughed with Mr Ford as if they shared a secret. 'Anyway, I'm not carrying it. Give it to Luke. It's his!'

'Mine?' I said, 'No, it's not mine.' thinking there must have been some terrible mistake.

'Yes, it is for you Luke. You see, I happen to know it's your birthday and I promised your mother we would give you a really happy birthday as she's away in France.'

I stood there in the shop amazed. I didn't know what to say. Mr Ford was smiling. 'Happy birthday!' he said.

'Well, open it!' said Guy.

I put it on the floor and between us we managed to get the paper off. Inside was a long flat box. I took off the lid and there was the most beautiful fishing rod complete with reel, hooks and a box of floats and weights. I had never handled a rod before and suddenly all this was mine. It was all just MARVELLOUS, SHINING and MINE!

'Come on boys!' said Mrs. Villiers 'I have a picnic to make before you go fishing. Let's get home.' After thanking Mr Ford, we piled all the stuff into the Landrover and set off back to Guy's house.

'You look as though you're off for a week.' laughed Guy's mother.

Then the phone rang. It was my Mum wishing me a Happy Birthday and telling me that Grandpa had come round, was feeling much better and they hoped to get him home in a few days. That was great news.

We finally set off to the river. I carried the picnic basket and my rod which Guy had to put together for me. He carried all the other tackle and his own rod. We ran down the slope to the water's edge. It was so still and quiet. It seemed as though we had the whole world to ourselves on that hot August day. We stood for a moment looking at the river.

'This way!' said Guy and ran over to what looked like a clump of trees and bushes. We pushed our way through and there, quite hidden, was a sort of shed.

'What's this?' I asked surprised.

'It's our boat-house.' said Guy.

'Boat-house? You've got a boat?' I said.

'Oh yes!' he said grinning at me.

'You said we were going fishing but you didn't say anything about a boat.'

'Well,' said Guy pulling open the doors, 'it's only a very little boat, at least mine is. My Dad's is a bigger one. Over there.' he pointed. 'It's called a slipper boat. We go out in that sometimes, all the family together and take picnics and go for miles downriver when it's not raining.'

I looked to where he pointed. There in the shadows of the shed I could see a long thin boat. It shone like red glass and had yellow leather seats.

I said, 'What a smashing boat!'

'This is mine.' said Guy turning back, and there was a neat little two man rowing boat. 'Take off your shoes and socks. We have to push her down the slipway into the water.'

'Her?' I said pulling off my sandals.

'Yes. All boats and ships are ladies! I've called her Lucy after my Grandmother.' We pushed her down to the water's edge and then into the water.

'Jump in while I hold her steady.' said Guy throwing in the rods and tackle bag. I got in with the picnic basket as he pushed her off and he jumped in too. We floated gently away from the edge.

'Is this the river?' I asked.

'Well, yes. I suppose it's all part of the river but this is just a backwater. If you look over to the right,' he pointed 'past that willow tree hanging in the water, there's a gap in the trees. If we follow the water round, there are six little islands. The main river is beyond all that. This part is our own private backwater and can't be seen from the river. It runs all along this bank for about a mile. Nobody comes here except us. The river gets very busy during the summer with lots of holiday boats. Here is a quiet sanctuary for birds and ducks. Lots of them nest on the islands. If we are very quiet, we may see the kingfishers. Dad said he thought we had three pairs nesting this last April. I've not seen them yet.'

We sat quietly. The water was like glass and so still. Where the sunlight broke through the leaves and down, down into the water, we could see the bottom of the pool.

'I can see right down there.' I said.

'Yes and if we sit quietly we may see Moby.'

'Who's Moby?' I asked.

'He's our pet trout,' said Guy 'He's huge and very old. Dad caught him last year and he and Uncle Chris weighed him. He was over 9 pounds.' Guy peered into the water. 'I can't see him.' he said. 'But if we tap the side of the boat he may come for food. 'We gently tapped the side of the boat and waited.

'He probably knows we are here anyway.' whispered Guy. 'Dad said he'd be able to hear any unusual sounds over a wide distance through the water. He says he's a very clever fish and he has no fear of us of course. We only feed him.'

We waited, gently tapping the boat and then suddenly, where a patch of sunlight fell on the riverbed, there was a flash of silver - a fish - a big fish.

'He's there!' said Guy getting quite excited. 'Look!'

'I see him' I said and watched the fish swimming slowly and very lazily at the bottom of the river under the boat. Guy had said he was a trout. I didn't know what sort of fish a trout was but he was a large fish.

'Throw a bit of bread into the water.' suggested Guy. 'He will come up to the surface and take it. He will sometimes take bread out of your fingers.'

I scattered a few small pieces of bread on the water and sure enough, he came up to the surface and took the pieces of bread into his mouth one at a time very slowly. None of the gobbling scramble we get when we feed the ducks. He was very well mannered for a fish and of course no one was threatening him or about to steal his food. He had all day, no need for hurry. He carefully cleared the last crumbs from the surface and deftly caught the few that were beginning to sink. He turned and looked at me!

'Hello Fish!' I said.

'Moby.' whispered Guy.

'Oh sorry! Moby.' I corrected myself. 'How are you?', and still he remained motionless looking at me. Perhaps he wanted more food. I felt I wanted to pat him on the head like a pet dog and then with a sudden flash of his tail and a splash of water he'd turned and dived to the bottom. We both gazed down into the water.

'He's there!' Guy pointed, 'feeding on something.'

Moby swam round on the bottom for a moment or two and then again with a strong swish of his tail he was gone, leaving behind a swirl of mud in the clear water. We sat in the boat gazing down watching the waterweed gently floating from side to side and the mud slowly settling to the bottom again. And then I saw it! In the mud, at least sticking out of the mud, was something that looked like a piece of bent metal, or was it wood?

'Can you see that down there?' I pointed.

'Where?'

'There! Look! Can you see that big brown pebble over to the right?'

'Yes I can. By that lump of green weed?'

'That's the one.' I said. 'Now further to the right. There is something sticking up out of the mud.'

'Oh yes. I see it.' he said. 'It's a lump of wood.'

'I don't think it is.' I replied. 'Anyway, I'm going down to get it. Hold the end of your rod in the mud beside it and I'll find it when I dive down there.'

I stripped off my shirt and clambered over the side into the water and hung on to the boat. I could reach the bottom and the water came to just below my shoulders.

'OK.' I said. 'Here goes!' And taking a deep breath I dived down to the riverbed. I had stirred up a lot of mud and couldn't see of course, but I followed guy's fishing rod and felt around with my fingers. Yes, I had it! It felt hard, cold and quite heavy as I pulled it out of the mud. Guy's face peered at me over the side.

'Did you get it?' he asked. I handed it to him and climbed back into the boat.

'It's metal.' I said grabbing a towel.

'Yes.' he nodded weighing it in his hand. 'It's heavy. Needs cleaning but what is it?'

He handed it back and I studied it. 'It may have been down there for years.' I said. It was made of a round metal rod bent in the shape of a horseshoe. There was a little wheel like a washer at the rounded end but instead of being smooth like a washer it had tiny points all round it like a star. It was loose enough to spin round. At least we decided it would spin round when it was cleaned up. It was all a bit corroded.

'We'll show it to Uncle Chris.' said Guy. 'He might know what it is or was. I think there's something broken off at this side. The metal here is a bit sharp.'

We ate our picnic and spent some time trying to clean the grime off our treasure. 'It could be very old and valuable.' mused Guy spinning the little wheel after scraping off some of the rubbish with a spoon from the picnic. He'd cleaned the 'thing' but hadn't done the spoon any good at all!

The rest of the day passed without any further excitement except that I caught a small fish with my beautiful new rod and line. We put him back in the water and set him free. 'Perhaps he'll grow up to be as big as Moby.' said Guy. I wonder if he ever did.

At 4 o'clock we put the boat back in the boathouse and climbed the hill to the manor.

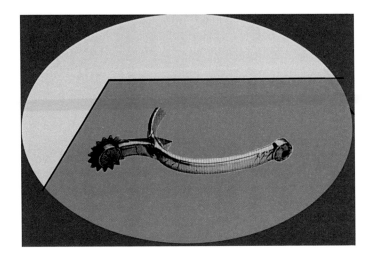

The broken spur

CHAPTER 4

SUE AND CHRISTOPHER

The Manor was very grand with its four tall chimneys. It also looked large standing on top of the hill making me feel very small. What a wonderful place to live and if the house could talk, what a great story it would have to tell, about all those people who had lived there over the years, perhaps knights in armour galloping across the hills, defending the house.

'Do you really have secret passages?' I asked Guy.

'Oh yes. Look at the house from here. We're looking at the side. What we call the front on the right overlooks the Thames down in the valley and over all those hills stretching away for miles. All the best rooms are at the front having the best views. Now, the left side is what we call the back. We went in that way yesterday through the kitchen. In olden days the family lived in all the posh rooms at the front and all the servants lived and worked at the back.'

'But back to the secret passages. Uncle Chris says that the front of the house is the oldest built in the time of Henry V111; the back was built on later and they built it to look exactly the same as the front. The roof's the same, the windows the same, a big door in the middle, and although the floors run right across the building, they left a space between the joining walls on the ground and first floors, giving us the secret passages. The top floor is all joined together and have no passages, at least, nobody has ever found any. We get into the passages from the library and out from a tiny door into what used to be the wine cellar right down under the house. There's another way out through a secret passage that goes underground and comes out in the wood over there.' He pointed.

'Dad says the passages were specially designed when the new bit was built on. One of my great-great-great-grandfathers, when he was about six, got himself shut in a secret room off the passage on the ground floor. Nobody has been able to find it since. They could hear him shouting behind the wall. It took them four hours to get him out. A gardener finally managed to touch the right panel in exactly the right way and the secret door opened.'

'But why, I wonder, would they build secret passages and secret rooms?' I asked.

'Well, Dad says in those days they could have been used to hide people or treasures and it's a secret way into the house to escape if you are being chased. It is said that spices, silks and brandy were smuggled from France up the Thames and hidden here by one of my ancestors who was a bit of a crook. They caught him in the end and he was hanged in London. I say! Wouldn't it be super if we could find the treasure? Let's go down the passages after tea.'

I thought I could do without tea. Would much rather explore the passages!

We put the hamper on the kitchen table but left our

fishing tackle in the porch. 'We'll clean it up after tea.' said Guy. 'We'd better hurry. Aunt Sue is doing food for us.'

We made our way over the hillside to the lodge. It was a long low house painted white, shining in the sunlight. It had two chimneys and pretty little bedroom windows peeping out from under a thatched roof. The back of the house was tucked into the hill but the front overlooked the hillside, the river below and the green hills beyond.

We walked into the porch which stored macs, wellies and fishing rods. I touched one of the fishing rods. 'They're Uncle Chris's.' said Guy kicking off his soggy sandals, so I did the same. We knocked and a lady's voice called us in.

'Hello Aunt Sue!' said Guy. 'This is my friend Luke.'

There was a most wonderful smell of baking and on a large wooden table in the center of the kitchen was something covered by a big white cloth. Aunt Sue was a small pretty lady with long blonde hair tied back with a ribbon. She had blue eyes and grinned at us both. I said 'Hello.'

'Hello boys!' she said. 'And a happy birthday, Luke! Go through both of you. Chris is on the terrace. We'll eat about half past five.'

'That's fine.' said Guy. 'But I'd like to show Luke the passages after tea if that's OK.'

'Why not ? Talk to Uncle Chris. He might go with you. He loves a bit of excitement.'

We walked through into a large lounge with quite a low ceiling; big soft armchairs were scattered about the room. One long wall seemed to be made completely, floor to ceiling, of glass windows overlooking the magnificent view. In the center were two glass doors standing wide open, leading onto a terrace. As we walked through the room we passed a carved wooden fireplace. It covered the chimneypiece up to the ceiling. The grate was big enough to burn logs - no fire that hot August day of course - instead, a vase filled with flowers stood in the hearth.

As I looked up at the carved scrolls and shapes above the mantelpiece, I saw again, right in the center, the family crest of two weapons carved into a shield, no paint this time, just shiny brownwood. A man's voice called from outside on the terrace 'Do hurry you two. I've been told by your Aunt not to touch this lemonade until you arrive and I'm dying of thirst.' The man with a smiling face and spectacles was sitting at a table under a big garden umbrella. He jumped up as we approached putting an arm round each of our shoulders.

'Good to see you, lads, and Luke, it's your birthday today I understand.'

'Yes, Sir.' I replied.

'Oh, No No! Don't call me Sir!' he grinned. 'Call me Chris. Now come on!' He gave us both a push towards the table. 'Grab a chair and let's drink.'

We sat around the table in the shade of the umbrella drinking Aunt Sue's special lemonade on that hot August day - my birthday! It was magic.

'I understand you've been fishing. Did you catch anything?' Chris asked.

'One little fish.' I replied. 'We put him back in the water.' 'We did find something though. Show Uncle Chris. Luke.'

I fished out our treasure and handed it to Chris.

'Goodness!' he exclaimed. 'Well. Where did you find this?'

'Luke found it.' said Guy. 'We'd just fed Moby. The sun was shining down into the water and he saw it sticking out of the mud.'

Chris turned it over in his hand. 'You've sharp eyes, Luke. Do you know what it is?' We both said no. 'It's part of a spur. A bit has snapped off. It would have been clipped onto a riding boot behind the heel. The rider would jab this sharp wheel into the horse's flank to make him go, run faster, hurry up.'

'Poor horse!' I said.

'Well yes.' said Chris. 'But there were times in war or perhaps when a man needed to get away in a hurry, a sharp dig in the horse's flank might have saved his life. Anyway, back to our spur. I think it could be silver. There are some markings here. Can't read them though. Too much incrustation from years in the river. However we'll get it cleaned up and I wouldn't be surprised if it dates back to the Civil War, about the 1640s. There were a lot of battles fought around here then and silver was used in some parts of the harnesses by rich horsemen. Possibly a Royalist Cavalier General of the King's Army.'

Civil War reminded me of history at school, Cavaliers and Roundheads fighting each other. I wished I had taken more notice at the time of the lessons. It had all happened so long ago that it just seemed like stories in a book; yet here was a bit of that story right here in my hand, a spur from a soldier's boot and suddenly it wasn't a story.

The Roundheads and Cavaliers in the books had been real people.

'What exactly was the Civil War?' I asked. 'How did it start? Didn't they chop off the King's head at the end of it?'

'Yes. They did execute the King at the end of the war in 1649 but so many things started the war.'

'Were Guy's family involved with the war?' I asked.

'I'm afraid they were. Have we got half an hour?" he said looking at his watch. 'And would you like to hear the story of the Civil War? Guy has heard some of it before of course.'

We both said 'Yes!'

'OK, so let's think where to begin.' said Chris.

CHAPTER 5

THE CIVIL WAR

'A civil war is a situation within a country when the people rise up against each other. In the English Civil War of the middle 1600s there were two sides. Some fought for King Charles l. They were the Royalists or Cavaliers, and others joined Oliver Cromwell and Parliament and were called Roundheads. Oliver Cromwell was an Army General and Member of Parliament for Cambridge.'

'We must go back to 1530 when Henry Vlll quarrelled (together with much of Europe) with the Pope and the ruling Roman Catholic Church in Rome. Everyone believed that Rome had too much power over the people. Henry decided that he would break away from Rome and he alone would rule his country, both the people and the church.'

'England became Anglican. However there were groups who believed the Anglican Church and their ideas of worship were too much like those of the Roman Catholic Church. They protested against Anglican ideas and became known as the Protestants. They wanted no Bishops or priests wearing glorious clothes and no lavish ceremonies in churches.'

'There was another group who believed the Protestants

did not go far enouugh in their separation from the Anglican Church. They also wanted no religious images, no rituals, no priests or bishops but they banned all singing and dancing and wore simple plain brown or black clothes. This group called themselves the Puritans. They lived a very simple life and were governed by elected elders of the people.'

'When Charles 1 was crowned in 1625 he was faced with this turmoil. Anglican, Protestants and Puritans were all quarrelling and fighting each other. Each believing that their idea of worship was the right one. The other lot's was rubbish.'

'Charles was a very religious man. He loved the Anglican Church; he loved the rituals, the pomp of the services, the wonderful garments worn by the priests and bishops and he enjoyed the singing. To the Protestants and Puritans this was too much like the Roman Catholic ideas. But Charles wanted the whole country to worship in the same way and as God had made him King, he said, he was in charge and all must obey him. He was not everybody's favourite person, and as many members of Parliament were Puritans he fell out with them and sent them all home.'

'Yet there were the Anglicans who enjoyed the old way of life. They enjoyed singing and dancing. These people had no wish to join the Puritans. They still believed that the King and the Church must rule the land.'

'The King then had a bright idea, a way of bringing everybody together. He set about writing a new prayer book with the help of his good friend, Archbishop Laud. They decided to try it out first in Scotland. He wanted to bring beauty and order to the their dour, dull way of worship. (The Scots were Presbyterians - another form of Protestants.)'

'What an awful mistake that prayer book was. They thought that the King was trying to reintroduce the Roman Catholic faith into Scotland and they rebelled. There were riots in the streets.'

'The King was advised to give up the idea of forcing the new prayer book on the Scots or else risk a rebellion. But, too late, the Scots, led by a number of powerful Scottish lords, had already rebelled and had formed a massive army of fighting clansmen all swearing to join together to oppose the new prayer book and any other bright ideas the King or Archbishop Laud may have had for Scotland. This was a novel idea for the clansmen who generally spent their time killing each other. This mighty Scottish force then attacked Berwick in Northeast England.'

'The King of course, refusing to change his mind, gathered an English army to defend England against the angry Scots in 1639. Some men from the North of England, joined the Scots and were all raring to go. But the men from the South of England were not so enthusiastic. They were short of weapons, had little food for themselves or their horses and very few supplies. They were camped in fields; it was cold and wet; they had no warm clothing or decent boots. Everybody complained from the most senior generals to the lowliest foot soldier. What was worse, they had little hope of being paid. The King had no money.'

'The English army began to melt away and go home. Charles was forced to make peace with the Scots. He went away, however, vowing to crush them next time.'

'Another friend of Charles was Thomas Wentworth

(Earl of Strafford). He told the King that he had to get more money from Parliament and also suggested that an Irish army should be recruited to help crush the Scots. The King recalled Parliament and demanded that they grant him money which they refused to do.'

'In London there were riots in the streets because Wentworth had suggested bringing the Catholic Irish over to England to kill Presbyterian Scots. With the Scots still invading the North of England the King managed to collect a raggle-taggle army to march against them. Again they were underpaid, underfed, ill equipped and in no mood for fighting and were defeated by the Scots at Newburn near Newcastle. The King again had to make terms with the Scots.'

'Parliament blamed Wentworth for the defeat calling him a traitor for encouraging the King to go to war anyway. Wentworth was arrested, taken to the Tower of London, tried, found guilty and beheaded.'

'Archbishop Laud was also a prisoner in the Tower of London and was blamed, together with his prayer book, for the strife in London and war against Scotland. He also lost his head. The King was now without most of his friends. Some had gone overseas out of harms way.'

'Parliament passed a law stating that the King was no longer in charge of the army, he was not allowed to tax the people without Parliament's permission and he must be wholly dependant on Parliament, allowing them to rule the land.'

'The King was furious. He said that, as King appointed by God, only he had the right to rule the land.'

'By now, the country and Parliament were both

divided. Many of the leading families were choosing which side they were on. It seemed the whole country was taking sides. There were riots in towns and villages all over the country, Parliamentarians fighting Royalists. The whole land was in uproar.'

'Parliament, trying to sort out the mess, accused the Queen of treason. To be convicted of treason in England meant beheading. '

'In the days that followed, London was in turmoil. The King, afraid for the safety of his family, sent the Queen to Holland with Mary, his eldest daughter, and the crown jewels which she hoped to sell to raise money.'

'In August 1642, the King moved to Nottingham and declared war on Parliament. Parliament then raised an army commanded by the Earl of Essex. Men and arms were mustered all over the country to join either King or Parliament. Civil war had begun. We were a nation at war with itself. The war would divide friends and families, often brothers and fathers and sons who found themselves fighting each other in different armies.'

'The King needed more men so he again sent to Ireland for help. This was a big mistake as I have said before. These men were Roman Catholics so here again was a situation where Irish Roman Catholics would be killing Protestant Englishman. Charles, as always, could see no wrong in this but he really had put his foot in it this time and the English never forgave him.

'The Civil War raged on over the years. Sometimes the Royalists would take a town from the Parliamentarians and sometimes the other way round. With all the fighting men away at the war only the old men, women and children were left to plough the fields, plant the seed and gather in the harvests. There was very little food and the towns and villages were expected to feed the armies of the King or of Parliament whichever happened to be there or passing through.'

'In 1645 many of the Parliamentarian generals were getting tired of war which seemed to go on and on year after year with nobody really winning. Oliver Cromwell decided to take command of the Parliamentary army himself and formed it into what became known as Cromwell's New Model Army. It was well clothed, well armed and trained into a powerful fighting force. As the King was losing more battles, many men left him to join this new model army. There at least they were fed and paid and had boots on their feet.

'The battle of Naseby was a particularly cruel fight for both sides. In the end, 4000 to 5000 Royalist troops were captured and several hundred killed. The King and some of his generals managed to escape but Cromwell captured the King's baggage train containing stores, food and ammunition. It also contained many secret coded letters and papers belonging to the King, copies of letters he had written to France, Holland and Ireland begging for money and men to help win his war.'

'When the papers were published the King lost the support of many Englishmen because it proved that he had been prepared to bring in foreigners to kill his own people many of whom were now Puritans.'

'The King decided that he would go to the Scots for help. They had been fighting alongside the New Model Army but recently had quarreled with Cromwell because they had not been paid. The Scots took the King north to Newcastle and for 8 months they tried to persuade him to change his religious ideas. But Charles refused. In the end the Scots got tired of him and agreed to hand him over to the Parliamentarians if Cromwell would pay them their back pay.

'The King was held a prisoner at Hampton Court but managed to escape to Carisbrooke Castle on the Isle of Wight. He was then made prisoner in the castle when it was realised that he had made secret plans with the Scots to invade England and return him to the throne.

'In 1649 Cromwell and Parliament took the King to London. He still refused to allow the more moderate religious ideas to be practiced throughout England, ideas which were somewhere between the harsh Puritans and the richer Church of England. They accused him of treason against his people. They called him a murderer, a traitor and a tyrant. They also called him a man of blood as he had declared war on Parliament, had tried to bring Scots, Irish and even continental soldiers to fight and kill Englishman.

'The King's trial began on 21st January 1649, and he, still believing himself to be appointed by God, asked how these mere mortal men dared to put him on trial? Throughout, he refused to answer the charges or to defend himself and on 27th, January, he was sentenced to death. On the 29th, a cold January morning, he was led out and beheaded.'

Guy and I both felt so sad for the King. Perhaps he was a silly man sometimes but I felt he could have been sent away, banished overseas perhaps and I said as much to Christopher.

'Yes. That would have been a kinder way of ending

the story.' he answered. 'But putting the King to death certainly stopped the war and the killing. '

'I suppose it did.' said Guy. 'It was very sad.'

'You said your family was involved.' I remarked. 'Were they for the King, Royalists, or for Parliament, the Roundheads?'

'They were on the Royalist side.' said Chris. 'But that's another story and I have a feeling that tea is ready. Aunt Sue has been busy laying out a feast.'

'OK you men.' she called. 'Come and get it!'

We trooped in off the terrace and oh boy! What a feast. Right in the middle of the table was a big birthday cake, the candles already lit.

'Happy birthday, Luke!' grinned Chris and they all sang "happy birthday".

I didn't know what to say except 'Thank you very much. This has been a super birthday.'

We tucked into bacon, eggs and chips, trifle and of course the birthday cake which was covered with icing and filled with jam and cream. I ate so much I couldn't move. Uncle Chris said he thought we would be too full of food now to go down the passages. Guy and I both shouted 'No! No! We're not.' Chris and Aunt Sue both laughed.

'OK then boys.' said Chris. 'To the passages! Let's go!'

CHAPTER 6

THE PASSAGES

Everyone, I soon discovered, referred to the secret passages as just 'The passages.'

'Passages,' explained Chris 'can mean any old passages and tends to keep the secret passages secret. Few people outside the family know about them.'

We crossed the hillside to the house and went in the back door into the hallway leading to the back stairs.

'The passages,' said Chris as we climbed the stairs, 'start on the second floor and run down through to the ground floor and then down into the cellars. 'Here,' he continued as we reached the top of the stairs and opened a large brown wooden door, 'is the library where they start.' We followed him into a very big room. The ceiling was high and most of the walls were covered with shelves filled with hundreds of books. The parts that were not covered with books were lined with brown wooden panelling. I ran my hand over a section of it. It was smooth and felt warm. Chris saw me and said, 'That is oak and was made and fitted at the time of King Henry V111 when this part of the house was built. Probably made from oak trees growing on the estate 450 years ago.'

Another huge fireplace which seemed to take up one whole wall was of brown carved wood, and there, above the mantelpiece, was the family crest of the two crossed weapons, exactly the same as on the front gate and in Chris' house.

'What a great big fireplace!' I remarked

'Yes.' said Chris 'We don't use the fire any more but you can stand right inside the empty grate and look up the chimney.' I did and I could see a tiny speck of daylight way up above me where the chimney opened up to the sky.

'I feel I could climb right up.' I said.

Chris laughed. 'Funny you should say that, Luke! In Victorian days the only way to sweep these large chimneys was to send up small children, smaller than you, with a brush to clean off all the soot. In fact there is a very famous book by Charles Kingsley called the Water Babies about a little boy chimney sweep, but enough chatter. Let's explore the passages.'

I climbed out of the fireplace and followed Chris and Guy to the right side of the chimney piece.

'The entrance to the passages is here tucked behind the chimney.' said Guy. And with that he placed his right hand flat on the center of a panel. Then, leaning firmly on the panel, turned his whole hand to the left. The panel moved, sort of turned. There was a click, then a whirring sound like a big clock about to strike and suddenly the whole block of paneling on his right became a door sliding open like a well-oiled spring. I jumped back quite scared because all I could see was a dark hole beyond this open door.

'Right!' said Chris. 'First things first. We put the "dog" against the door.' And, lifting a life sized bronze model of a spaniel, he propped open the door. The dog was sitting looking up as though waiting for someone to throw him a ball. He had long ears and a beautiful face. I patted him on the head. Chris smiled 'Meet Henry!' he said 'Nobody goes into the passages without first leaving Henry on guard holding open the door. People would now know there is someone in the passages and should the cellar door be blocked, which it once was by a fallen tree, you can get back this way. The spring lock on the door can be opened from the inside but it is very difficult. Second thing, we need the torches.' He opened a cupboard and took out three torches and handed them round.

Whilst Chris had been talking I had peeped through the open door into the passage. It was black dark and cold air seemed to hit me in the face. It was really spooky. I might tell you, I was more than a bit scared.

'Torches working?' said Chris. I think he knew I was scared because he put his arm around my shoulder. 'Right! Let's go!'

Leading the way he set off, we two following. Once the torches were on of course it was not quite so frightening but there was still that draft of cold air as though there was a window open. There was a strange smell, too, of old houses or old damp books.

As though reading my thoughts Chris said 'It always smells like this. Not much air passes through when it is all closed up and I feel it's a bit ghostly.'

'It's the silence I guess. I always feel there is someone watching me.' said Guy. 'It's so still and if we turn off our torches it's completely dark, no windows, no daylight, just black darkness.' he giggled. 'It's really exciting!'

'There are brackets on the walls in places to hold candles but they would have been a dangerous fire risk. All this wood would burn like tinder, so we carry torches.'

Chris went first then Guy and I followed. Looking ahead, the passage was well lit by our torches but I was very aware of the darkness that was behind; it seemed to be following me.

Chris was busy explaining how the passages had been built. It looked just like a long narrow corridor and he described how it was formed between two halves of the house. The walls of the passages were beautifully panelled in dark brown wood as in the library. The floor was covered with thick wooden floorboards which creaked a bit. We both wore sandals and Chris was still wearing his slippers so our feet didn't make much noise. Reaching the end of the passage we came to a spiral stairway built of brick or stone.

'This stairway has actually been built into, and down through the wall to the floor below.' explained Chris. 'It was constructed when the outside wall was built so as you see, these passages were not caused by a fault in the design or because the builder forgot to join the two halves together. The whole thing was planned and very cleverly planned.'

'Wish I knew why.' said Guy.

Holding tightly to a metal handrail fastened to the wall we all clambered down the steps to the floor below which opened up from the end of the stairs onto another passage. Here as before the walls were covered with the dark brown panels and again we walked along a creaky wooden floor going back the other way.

'These floors do creak a bit.' remarked Chris. 'But considering it was laid down at the time of Queen Elizabeth 1 in about 1570 I guess we're lucky it's only creaking. There is a hard stone floor underneath it of course just as there are hard stone walls behind these lovely panels.' He tapped the walls with his knuckles. We did the same and it made a hollow sound as though there was an empty space behind it.

'We think there may be hidden rooms somewhere along these passages. A Great-great - oh I don't know how many greats -grandfather of Guy's, as a small boy many years ago, actually found one by accident and got shut inside. Somewhere, we think on the ground floor, but it's never been found since he was rescued, although generations of Villiers have tapped, knocked and pushed these panels in the hope of finding it.'

'We are now on the ground floor and this staircase is exactly the same as the other one and takes us down into the cellars.' As he spoke I could see we were approaching the end of the passage and ahead yet another stairwell falling down into the darkness.

'Down we go!' said Chris lighting up the stairs with his torch. 'Hang on tight to the rail.'

'It's a bit like a well.' I said feeling distinctly worried and hoping I didn't fall.

''Tis a bit.' laughed Chris 'But so long as you hang on tight and go carefully you are quite safe and I promise there is no water at the bottom.'

Down, down we went. All around us was the light

from the torches but above us, it was now totally black and the darkness still seemed to be following us down. I was very pleased to reach the bottom and found we were in a small stone-walled room. Against the wall was a cupboard built of heavy dark brown wood. It looked a bit rough. Chris noticed me looking at it. 'That cupboard is also made of oak and was probably made in the early 1600s. Now,' he said, 'as you see we have a stone room. This door on my left leads to the cellars.'

It was small. Even I had to bend to get through into the cellar.

'Now, come back here and close the door, Luke. You'll see a bit of magic.' said Chris. 'Hold my torch please.' He removed a large pin from the back of the wooden cupboard. He took hold of it and swung the left side of the cupboard away from the wall. The right side corner was still attached to the wall by a big metal hinge but most surprising of all, there was another tiny door hidden behind the cupboard. He opened it and we all crawled through on our hands and knees. On the other side was yet another passage, quite low. Chris who was almost 6ft tall had to bend his head but Guy and I managed to walk upright.

'People in days gone by tended to be shorter than we are today.' said Chris walking ahead. 'I guess this was made for those little people.'

We followed him through the passage coming finally to a set of stone steps cut into the thick wall and topped by a wooden door. Guy ran on ahead and unbolting the door pushed it open. The daylight and the sunshine flooded in and clambering out we sat on a patch of grass surrounded by trees and bushes. The warm sunshine filtered through the leaves. It felt really good after those dark passages.

'Well, Luke. What did you think of our passages?'

'I think they're great. But they were really scary!' I replied.

'Guy doesn't often go down by himself but it will be fun for the two of you to explore them.'

'Why were there two ways out of that little stone room?' I asked.

'Just to confuse the people chasing you I guess. They would have expected you to have gone through into the cellar when, in fact, you could have come this way perhaps hiding in this passage here until nightfall, then escaping down the hill to the river and be miles away while your pursuers were still searching the cellar. The more I see of these passages the more sure I am that they were built as escape routes. I wish I knew who these people were or why they needed this wonderful secret way out which is still as good today as it was when it was constructed.'

'Come now, we must get back.' he said. 'Aunt Sue will be thinking we are locked in and come looking for us.'

We wandered back through the passages locking doors behind us as we went. It was really not so scary the second time but as Guy had said, it was so very quiet. The dog Henry was still faithfully holding open the secret panel door. He was carefully put back against the wall and the door closed. I looked up again at the crest carved over the fireplace. 'Guy's Mum said those swords were part of the treasure that was lost.' I said to Chris, hoping he would tell me something about this treasure.

'Yes they were.' he replied 'but I'm not sure the treasure was lost. It may have been sold. Perhaps the family needed the money or perhaps it was taken to France when the family escaped after the Civil War. It might have been stolen, I suppose, but the last time it was known to be here in the possession of the family was in 1638. That was about the time King Charles tried to push his new prayer book on the Scottish people. We have an inventory listing all the items of the treasure dating back to that date.'

'Maybe it was given to the King to sell. He was always short of money.' suggested Guy.

'Maybe.' said Chris.

'Did you enjoy the passages?' asked Aunt Sue as we walked back through their kitchen. 'They're a bit frightening, aren't they?'

'Yes a bit.' I said 'but exciting.'

'Yes.' she replied. 'As a little girl my brother and I spent many happy hours in there inventing games of spies and escaping into the woods, or being highway men creeping back into the house with our loot. We also spent hours trying to find the secret room off the passages - never found it unfortunately. No treasure. No nothing. I'm sure they'll find it one day. I feel sure it's here somewhere.'

'Did you live there?' I asked surprised.

'Yes all my life.' she laughed, 'When we were children our Grandmother lived here in this cottage and we as a family lived in the manor. The passages were our playrooms. We were very lucky!'

I was still wondering about the treasure. 'I wonder what

happened to that treasure?' I said. 'You said the family were Royalist for the King. What happened to them?'

'That's another story.' said Chris. 'Come round tomorrow, if you like, and I'll tell you about the de Villes of the 1630s.'

'How do you know so much about them?' I asked wondering whether anybody knew anything about my ancestors so far back.

Chris smiled. 'We have a lot of information about the family written down as it happened by the family vicar and by the de Ville's secretary. We also have letters from friends and stories told by the servants of what happened in those days. Somebody gathered all this information together and finally bound it into a book. They all vanished you know, the whole family. "Vanished off the face of the earth!" said one servant at the time. Pop round tomorrow and I'll find the book and tell you about them.'

I wanted to go on with the story then but we had to go. We thanked Aunt Sue for a super supper, wished Chris good night and wandered back over the hillside to the manor. It was a warm beautiful evening and we were both reluctant to go indoors just yet. We sat down on the soft warm grass both thinking about the Civil War.

'How can a whole family vanish?' I said.

'Don't know.' said Guy. 'I've heard the story before but I won't tell you about it. We'll let Uncle Chris tell us the story tomorrow.'

As I lay in my cosy bed at the top of Guy's house that night I decided it was quite the most wonderful birthday I had ever had. My new fishing rod, fishing from Guy's boat, meeting Moby the fish, finding the broken spur and the wonderful story of the Civil War; finally, that trip down the passages not forgetting the birthday supper and the birthday cake.

Guy's father had come home from London with his Mother that evening. He was a palaeontologist and worked at a Museum in London all week lecturing and studying fossils, only getting home at weekends. He was very tall and had grey blue eyes and dark curly hair, not a bit like his sister. He took us across to their little wood and showed me their three owl nesting boxes where the owls had reared four chicks in the spring.

Henry

Looking through the open window at the clear starry sky I could hear the owls as I fell asleep.

CHAPTER 7

SATURDAY

The next day was Saturday, great excitement. Guy's Dad, Chris, Andrew and Timothy were all going to excavate the land beyond the barn behind the farm. Guy's Dad said there were possibly some Anglo-Saxon buildings there; Guy and I could go and help dig if we wished. We were each given a trowel and a large soft paintbrush and instructed how to gently scrape away the hard topsoil then brush it away. We then had to gather all the soil that we had loosened into a bucket which would be pushed through a sieve by a gang of senior students from the local school, who'd come to help.

The men carefully lifted off the green turf and we all set to work scraping. It was hard work and made our necks ache; it was very hot. It was a gloriously sunny day and suddenly Guy whispered in my ear 'I would love a swim!'

'Oh! So would I!' I said.

'Let's go!' he said getting up and brushing the dirt off his knees. 'We're going for a dip in the river, Dad.' he called.

'OK boys!' his Dad answered. 'But stay in the shallows and don't go out into the main river.'

'No, Dad, we won't.'

We ran to the little pools where we had fished the day before and, stripping off our t-shirts, plunged into the clear cool water. Afterwards we sat on the bank in the warm dappled shade to dry off.

'Wonder if they've found anything at the dig?' said Guy, 'Things have been found before, dug up by the plough, and Andrew found a broach pin and some coins. He says there would have been a farm, maybe even a village, on the area when the Normans conquered it and the de Villes took over the land. The Normans would be the new rulers but they would need the people to work the land, so I suppose the Saxons would be allowed to live there as before.'

'They might find a horde of treasure.' I suggested.

'They might, let's go back and see.' said Guy, jumping up. 'Anyway, it must be lunchtime. I'm starving.'

As I fastened my sandal I realised that the buckle was loose. Perhaps Liz would stitch it on for me. We children wore leather sandals then, which had a little buckle at the side a bit like a small belt buckle. A strap went across the foot and was fastened by the buckle. These buckles often came loose and even came off at times and had to be stitched back in place with strong cotton.

The diggers had unearthed a wall and had found lots of bits of pottery which Timothy was very excited about! It didn't look much to me but then at eleven years old it was hard to get excited about a few bits of broken plate.

'Did you find any human bones or any treasure?' asked Guy.

'Fraid not; not yet anyway but we're just packing up for lunch. We'll try again this afternoon.' laughed Andrew.

'Andrew is a anthropologist.' said Guy as we walked back to the house.

'What's that?' I asked.

'A sort of archeologist but he studies people and how they live. He also manages the farm. He says he gets paid for farming.'

Chris went back to the lodge for his lunch saying 'I'll see you boys at about four o'clock. OK?'

'Yes please.' said Guy. We then all piled into the big kitchen at the manor for a sandwich lunch. After lunch we went down to the dig again but at four o'clock exactly we knocked on the back door of the lodge.

'Hello boys.' said Aunt Sue as she let us in. 'Chris is on the terrace.'

We walked out into the sunshine.

'Ah good, you've arrived! Did they find anything in the trench?'

'Only a few more bits of pottery but they've uncovered more of a wall.'

'Tim thinks it's almost surely a house or what's left of it.' said Guy. 'And Andrew was happy. He thought he may have found an ancient rubbish tip (he called it a midden) which he said will tell us a lot about the people who lived there before Willy the Conk.'

We sat down at the table and Chris looked at us and grinned. 'Well - all ready for the next instalment? Guy has heard all this before of course. Did you tell Luke any of it?'

'No.' I answered. 'He wouldn't tell me anything!'

'Well you see, I like hearing the story myself so I didn't spoil it for Luke.'

'Good.' said Chris. 'Well here goes. This is the book

I told you about yesterday. It's full of knowledge about the de Ville family just before and during the Civil War. It contains lots of information, and also gives us an idea how people lived in those days.'

'The de Villes who were living here then were a rich and happy family. They owned the manor and had lots of servants and people to run the farm and the estate. The Civil War would change all that but let's start at the beginning.'

'Sir Guy de Ville had, like his ancestors, been born in the manor and apart from the time he spent away at school, had lived there all his life. We start this story about 1620. He was married and he and his wife had three children - the eldest, Guy of course. All these Guys get a bit confusing but as I have said before, the eldest son has always been called Guy. His second son was Harry and his daughter was called Rebecca.'

'Now, Luke, come over here.' Chris walked to the side of the terrace and pointed. 'Look across the valley and up the next hillside. You see a line of trees?'

'Yes.'

'They are roughly at the edge of this estate and the next one, which belonged to a family called Bruce. Donald Bruce was a Scotsman who had come down to England with James 1 and was a neighbour and friend of our de Villes.'

'The Bruces had two boys. The youngest son was William, and Daniel, the eldest who was the same age as Harry de Ville. Harry and Daniel became great friends, a bit like you two, although all five children spent much of their childhood years together. Their fathers decided to employ a private tutor and so all five were there learning to read, write and calculate (arithmetic or maths to you!) up in one of the attic rooms here at the manor. That room is still called the schoolroom.'

'Yes it is!' said Guy. 'I often wondered why a bedroom was called a schoolroom!'

'Life went on.' continued Chris. 'These five children lived a carefree life on the hillsides. They were all excellent horsemen and women, for Rebecca refused to let the fact that she was a girl allow her to fall behind the boys in anything. In fact she made her mother cut her hair short and wore breeches (Trousers. Possibly one of the first women in history to wear trousers.) and boots like her brothers, asking how she was expected to keep up with the boys with a gown flapping around her ankles. I guess we would call her a tomboy today. They were also taught how to use a sword, how to fire a pistol and were all good archers.'

'As they grew older leaving their childhood behind they were still the best of friends. Rebecca de Ville eventually married Daniel Bruce much to both families' delight. Guy, the eldest de Ville, had gone to London to become a lawyer but had died of smallpox when he was twenty. This left Harry now the eldest son, heir to the de Ville fortune and a staunch Royalist like his father.'

'Daniel Bruce, Harry's best friend and now his sister's husband, went into Parliament having been elected a Member of Parliament for this area. Perhaps you can even now see this story evolving, Luke?'

'Yes I can.' I said.

Chris continued. 'When the old King James 1 died,

Charles, his son, was crowned King becoming Charles 1 and here begins the years of tragedy that led up to the Civil War we talked about yesterday.'

'At the outbreak of war Daniel Bruce sided with Parliament and eventually became a general in Oliver Cromwell's army. Harry de Ville fought with the King also becoming a general. So there they were these two great friends in different armies which were fighting each other. Harry with the Royalists or Cavaliers for the King, Daniel fighting for the Parliamentarians or Roundheads. However during those war years, if ever they were at their homes together, they would meet as they had always done, the best of friends. At home, they agreed there would be no war, and there never was a war between them. Fortunately they never met on a battlefield and so were spared the horror of possibly killing each other.'

'Daniel had said that he would fight for Parliament because he believed they were right and the King was wrong. But he would never become a Puritan.'

'At the end of the war after the King had been beheaded in 1649, Cromwell began to look around for the leading Royalists who had fought for the King, calling them traitors. He had a number of them on his list. Many had escaped to France or Holland or were just in hiding. Harry, who had fought bravely throughout the war and had proved to be a very able general, was on Cromwell's list for two reasons. First for being a Royalist general and second because it was thought he had hidden King Charles' eldest son here at the manor and had also helped him to escape to France. In fact it was not the Royal Prince at all but the seventeen-year-old son of another royalist general who, having been fatally wounded, begged Harry to look after his son. Unfortunately, one of the servants here at the Manor, was a spy for Cromwell and, thinking this boy was the Prince, had reported the matter to Cromwell.'

'Hey!' I said. 'He was probably hidden in the passages.'

'Very likely or perhaps in one of those secret rooms we've never found.' said Chris. 'But Prince or not, Harry de Ville was on Cromwell's most wanted list and so he ordered General Daniel Bruce to arrest Harry and bring him to London.'

'This was a terrible blow to Daniel. Harry and he had been like brothers and he was even married to Harry's sister. They had managed to stay out of each other's way right throughout the war and now it was all over, he had been ordered to go and arrest Harry, accuse him of treason, and escort him to the Tower of London for trial. I imagine he must have felt pretty sick. Rebecca was terribly upset. Cromwell seemed to be taking a nasty delight in the situation knowing that these two men had grown up together; but it was also thought he was punishing Daniel for not changing his religion.'

'Daniel had to do something. He had to warn Harry but which of the servants could be trusted? He knew many were now puritans and some had fought with Cromwell. Then, he remembered Jacob. Jacob was over seventy and had been working for the Bruce family all his life. Although now retired to a tiny cottage on the Bruce estate he still took a lively interest in the family. He had taught Daniel to ride when he was a small boy and had watched all five children, Bruces and de Villes, grow up. If they had ever needed anything they had always gone to Jacob. Daniel felt sure that Jacob could be trusted and Jacob could read and write.

'He waited for Jacob outside church that following Sunday and pushed a note into Jacob's hand asking him to warn Harry de Ville that he was coming to arrest him in two days time. Daniel knew he had to wait for his escort to arrive from Reading the next day and by then it would be too late in the day to set off for London with his prisoner. This hopefully would give Harry time to escape. (However Daniel was in for a shock). For the arrest he would be provided with a troop of six fully armed Roundhead cavalry soldiers, one mounted sergeant and a Major Willis also heavily armed. Cromwell was taking no chances should the prisoner try to escape.'

'Daniel set off with his escort early on the Tuesday morning. It must have been a sad journey from his own house, across this hillside where they had ridden together so often as children, here to the manor, knowing he had to arrest his friend. The Major hammered on the door. A servant answered and was asked to inform his master that officers of the government had arrived to arrest him and take him to London on a charge of treason. To Daniel's horror, Harry appeared at the door apparently knowing nothing about his possible arrest. Daniel said afterwards, he had wondered what had happened to his warning letter and what had happened to Jacob? Had he betrayed his trust or worse, had he been caught by Cromwell's spies?'

'Harry sent a servant to saddle his horse and invited Daniel and the officers in. They refused. Daniel, I'm sure, could not look his friend in the face. He could not understand why Harry had not escaped two days ago.

Had he not received his warning? Daniel had risked his own life to send it. What ever had happened?'

'Later Harry came out with his manservant who was carrying two loaded saddlebags. Harry's wife, his 10-year-old son Guy, his daughter Violet and his baby son Edward carried by the nursemaid, all followed Harry out of the house.'

'Harry, dressed for the journey, handed Daniel his sword saying "Take good care of it my friend, it belonged to my father. Now I'm ready. I have one small favour to ask. Please permit me with my family to go to the chapel to pray together and say my goodbyes to them there." Daniel agreed and everybody trooped across the grounds to our little family chapel and went inside, the two servants, Harry, his wife and children. Daniel and his troop stayed outside and waited.'

'I have no idea how long they waited there. Quite some time I imagine. Eventually, Daniel opened the chapel door and the Major, the Sergeant and all the troopers followed him in. There was no one there! The little church was empty, absolutely silent and to this day we have no idea where they went!'

'"HOW CAN ANYBODY LOSE FOUR ADULTS AND THREE CHILDREN IN A TINY CHAPEL?" This is what the furious Cromwell asked, but Daniel, though delighted his friend had gone, was just as puzzled as any one. Fortunately he had his Major and the rest of the troop to back him up when he said that they had apparently vanished. He asked Jacob days later if he had managed to deliver his message to Harry. Jacob had assured him that he had. Jacob said that Harry had thanked him for his bravery in delivering the note and said "EVERYTHING

IS IN HAND." Harry was eventually forgiven by Cromwell and was allowed to return to Parliament.'

'Some months later, Daniel had heard that the de Villes had reached France safely and were living outside Paris with friends. However there was a sad ending to the story. Harry, his wife and two eldest children plus the servants all died of the plague. The only survivor was baby Edward. He came back to England when Charles 11 was crowned in 1660. Charles gave Edward back this house and land which Cromwell, in his fury at the family's escape in 1649, had confiscated. He lived here in peace for the rest of his life. But we have more evidence of earlier family history which turned up a few years ago. I'll show you.' He grinned at Guy.

'It seems very sad that they had managed to escape Cromwell only to die in France of the plague.' I said.

'Sad, yes, but many people died of the plague in those days. At least Edward finally got back here to continue the de Villes' story.'

CHAPTER 8

AN OLD BOX

Chris got up and went into the lounge and came back a couple of minutes later placing a beautiful box on the table. It was twice the size of a shoe box, made of wood covered in leather and held together by metal straps.

'Is that old?" I asked.

'Oh yes,' said Chris. 'and you'll never guess where we found it!' He looked at Guy. 'You tell him.' he said laughing.

'Well.' Guy took a deep breath. 'It was about two years ago, my tenth birthday December 22nd. There was a terrible storm. It was blowing down trees all over the estate, in fact all over the area. People were losing rooves and we had a barn blown into the Thames. But it also blew a chimney pot off the house. Most of it fell onto the roof taking the tiles with it but some fell down the chimney, bringing a load of soot with them, fetching up all over the library floor. Andrew, who was studying in the library at the time, said it was probably Father Christmas making an early call and perhaps we should send someone up in case he was stuck there, but Mum wasn't best pleased. There was a terrible mess. Andrew's dog, Mark, who was sitting on the hearthrug at the time must have thought the sky had fallen in. He rushed down stairs and out of the house covered with soot and dust. We couldn't find him for ages.' Chris laughed.

'However,' he continued. 'we got the builder to replace

the roof tiles and mend the chimney. But in the course of his work the builder looked up the chimney from the library fireplace just as you did yesterday, Luke, and discovered, about five feet up inside, a mass of bricks had been pulled away from the chimney wall by the weight of rubbish falling down from above. The fall had exposed a metal door set into the chimney wall. The bricks that had fallen from the wall had, it seemed, only been placed there to cover this metal cupboard door. When we finally opened the door we found this box inside that very secret cupboard. You can imagine the excitement. We thought it might contain some of the treasure.'

'Or at least tell us where it is. But it didn't.' said Guy.

'No. It didn't.' agreed Chris. 'But it did contain a lot of written information about the family through the centuries.'

He opened the box. 'It contained this list of the family treasure.'

A Crusader's sword.

A Scimitar.

A Salt.

A jeweled headdress and a matching necklace.

A Communion Plate. 2 Gold Candlesticks.

A Chalice, gold and jeweled. A gold Altar Cross.

20 silver Forks.

20 gold Spoons.

Silver Buckles.

20 gold trenchers.

12 Apostle spoons.

'The list is dated 1648 - just before the King was

executed. I guess the treasure was all hidden for safety.'
Chris said.

'We also have lots of information about the family, the buying and selling of land, names of people who lived and worked here on the estate way back in the 15 and 16 hundreds. They once entertained Queen Elizabeth 1 and we have a list of what they cooked for her dinner and what it cost. Chris was flicking through papers as he was talking. He looked up. 'She was staying elsewhere and only came here for a meal. Judging by the cost of one meal, I reckon they were pleased she didn't stay longer. She did have a nasty habit of inviting herself to stay at rich landowners castles and manors. Perhaps this place was considered a little too small for her as she always brought all the Lords and Ladies of the court with her. Perhaps it was after her visit that they decided to extend the house.'

'But also,' continued Chris, 'we have the story of a young man called Guy who lived here in a house on this spot in about 1160, but that house probably looked more like the house you see in that drawing downstairs. He was the young man who went to the Crusades with his cousin and took part in a terrible battle.'

Chris lifted out a pile of what looked like very thick paper. 'Here is Guy's story. It was written on vellum by a priest called Friar Pierre, Peter. It was written in Norman-French, the language spoken by the nobles. However somebody rewrote it in 1620 translating it into English. Probably found it dropping to bits. He must have had a terrible job trying to translate it but also trying to read the terrible writing of Friar Pierre. And now I have re-rewritten it again. It has taken me over two years and I'm hoping to turn it into a book. I'll read you the manuscript of Guy's story and I'll also tell you a bit about the Crusades but,' he grinned. 'that's another story for another day. Have you seen our little chapel, Luke?' I said no. 'Come on.' said Chris, 'I'll walk over with you and perhaps you two, between you, can solve the four-hundred-year-old mystery, HOW DID THE DE VILLE FAMILY VANISH?'

The chapel stood on the hill at the far side of the wood hidden from the house by the trees. It was a small rectangular building and had a square stone tower at one end. Built of local Cotswold stone and flint and, depending on the time of day and the light from the sun, the walls could look pink and even golden in the evening sunlight.

We opened the heavy wooden door and walked into the cool quiet chapel. Chris' footsteps echoed, breaking the silence. The walls were stark white. The only decoration was a number of old army flags hanging on poles way up near the roof, quietly waiting perhaps, for a soldier to come and collect them and carry them again into some long forgotten battle. They waved gently as the draft from the door caught them.

There were two stained glass windows down each side of the building. Chris explained that one was in memory of men and women killed in the First World War and opposite was one in memory of those killed in the Second World War. The flags, he said, belonged to old army regiments some of them hundreds of years old. The other windows were pictures of people, probably Saints, all made from hundreds of brightly coloured pieces of glass, very old, probably dating back 400 years. The sun, shining through on one side, cast a rainbow of colours across the floor and across the altar at one end. A reflection from a dark red cloak, worn by a figure carrying a little lamb, looked like a bloodstain on the floor. I pointed this stain out to Chris. He smiled.

'And that stain moves across the floor as the sun goes across the window. It's quite eerie! Sometimes, as the evening sunlight shines through the waving branches of the trees, that red shadow is scattered into pieces across the font and looks like flames.'

The altar at the far end of the chapel was a long wooden table covered by a white cloth edged with red. The cloth reached to the floor all round. There was a small cross standing in the middle of the altar flanked by two silver candlesticks. Embroidered on the front of the white cloth in gold was the family crest of the two crossed weapons.

The seating was rows of plain wooden benches. 'Not very comfortable seats.' I remarked.

'They are not but they were put there by the puritans who didn't allow comfortable seats.' Chris sat down on one of the benches. 'Right now, Mr Sherlock Holmes and Dr. Watson, see if you can tell us how the de Ville family managed to vanish into thin air. Remember one of the three children was a tiny baby and it's very hard to stop a baby crying and a crying baby makes a lot of noise. You can imagine it echoing round these walls.'

Guy and I walked right round the solid white walls. There was only one small archway at the back end which opened onto a small square room. A spiral stone stairway snaked its way up and round and round against the wall going up and up to the top of the tower. A rope was hanging down from the top but was pinned against the wall out of the way.

'What is that rope?' I asked.

'It's the bell rope.' answered Guy.

'Does the bell ring?'

'Oh yes.' said Guy. I would have loved to have had a go and pulled it.

'The chapel is still in use.' said Chris following us into the tiny room. 'We have weddings, christenings and funerals when we ring the bell and it is rung on Sunday mornings before the service.'

I peered up the stone stairs. 'Perhaps they escaped up there?' I suggested.

'And where do you suppose they went then? They couldn't fly and they certainly didn't jump. Go up. Have a look.' he suggested. 'But hold on to the metal handrail. I don't want you breaking your necks.'

We clambered up the small stone steps that spiraled up into the tower. Almost at the top we came to the bell hanging on its great wooden supports anchored to the wall, the rope falling down to the ground level. We climbed up a little further to a small door, which opened onto the parapet at the top of the square tower, and clambered out. We stood there, breathless from the climb, overlooking the countryside which stretched for miles and miles all around. Chris came up behind us also out of breath.

'Well, Luke! See what I mean?'

'Yes,' I agreed. 'There's no way of escape from here.'

'Anyway,' said Chris peering down. 'The troopers

were down below there on the paving around the entrance door.'

Later, as Guy and I wandered back to the manor, we turned and looked again at the pretty little chapel.

'They were very clever!' muttered Guy. 'They got clean away. Fetched up in France. Probably got a boat down the Thames.'

'Yes,' I said, 'we know that, but how did they get out of the church?'

CHAPTER 9

MORE TALES - THE CRUSADES

We had agreed to go and see Chris on Sunday afternoon.

'Come in!' he shouted, 'I'm just getting all this paperwork in order.' He was sitting at the table in the lounge surrounded by documents. The glorious sunshine of the past week had gone. It was raining and a cold wind was blowing over the hillside. We sat curled up in the soft comfy chairs and waited for him to begin.

'I have here those three copies of the story of the first Guy, that boy who went to the Middle East, which became known as Outremer at the time of the Crusades. This one is by the Friar Peter.' He pointed to one of the piles of scripts. 'It was written carefully and probably very slowly in ancient ink with, perhaps, a quill pen made from a goose feather on goatskin just as Guy dictated the story, and as I told you, it came out of the box which fell out of the chimney.'

'This one,' He held up another book. 'is the copy of that story translated from the Norman-French by somebody in about 1610-20, also out of that box. And THIS,' he held up a bound manuscript. 'is my copy of the 1600 one. It's taken me two years to produce and I hope to get it published eventually. We might get the roof replaced if it sells!' he laughed.

'You asked about the Crusades, Luke. In 1095 the

Saracens and Turks attacked the Empire of Byzantium whose capital was Constantinople. They had been attacking for years and had already taken a lot of the land belonging to the Byzantine Empire He handed us a map. 'You can see Byzantium and Constantinople. We now call it Istanbul.'

'The Emperor of Byzantium had finally panicked. His beautiful, rich land along the warm sunny Mediterranean coast with its schools, universities, hospitals, libraries, magnificent cathedrals and a wealthy merchant people, was unable to defend itself, for although it had good city walls it had a very small army. He sent a hasty message to the Pope in Rome for help. The Pope ruled and governed the religious life of the people in Northern Europe. Their ceremonies were performed in Latin, the language of the old Roman Empire, so they were called Latins.'

'Now the Byzantine people and those living along the Mediterranean coast on islands such as Cyprus and Crete were Greek Orthodox, not governed by Rome or the Pope. For years these two powerful Christian peoples had worshipped in their own way and had quarreled with each other, both believing that their form of worship was the true one and that the other lot were rubbish. For years they refused to even talk to each other. So, when the Pope got this call for help from the Greek Emperor of Byzantium he was delighted. At last this rival upstart who had dared to call himself the Holy Roman Emperor was in need of Roman Latin help. The Pope thought he himself might eventually sit on the Byzantium throne thus making himself leader of all faiths, both Greek and Latin.'

'He called a big meeting at a place called Claremont in

France in 1095. Thousands attended from senior bishops to humble priests, knights, barons, merchants, farmers and peasants all gathered and listened to the Pope as he told them of the horrible things the barbarians had done to the Byzantiums. "Go!" he begged them. "Go and save your eastern brothers who are being slaughtered by these infidels". For those who obeyed his call he promised that all their sins would be forgiven and anyone who was unfortunate enough to get himself killed would go straight to heaven. He also said that all those who went, must wear a red cross stitched to their clothes representing the cross of St. George. There was a terrible shortage of red cloth for years afterwards! "Oh yes!" continued the Pope. "And when you've sorted out Byzantium just pop over to Jerusalem and save your brothers there." That was not a good idea. Jerusalem was a large city of many races and religions who had been living quite peacefully together for 400 years and nobody needed saving.'

'Thousands upon thousands applied and all went marching across Europe wearing their red crosses. They took their women and children with them would you believe! Some went by sea, many overland by horse, but the peasants walked - by the thousand.'

'The poor emperor, Alexius of Byzantium, was horrified. He had only wanted a couple of regiments to help defend his city walls or even some recruits, volunteers perhaps, to swell his own army. He would pay well. But he seemed to be getting the whole of the Latin world, their families as well. He couldn't cope. He couldn't feed them or their animals; he couldn't house them and of course didn't speak their languages. It was a disaster. He had hoped that they would help him regain the territory he had lost but they came expecting him to help take Jerusalem. They arrived by the thousand in great waves. He did his best to send them on their way to Jerusalem before the next lot arrived, particularly as the barons leading the various groups, were probably at war with each other anyway.'

'The Crusaders carried on across Asia Minor and I'm afraid in 1099 they did "save" Jerusalem. It was a bloodbath. They massacred many hundreds of men, women and children, whatever nationality or religion, because after all, these people all wore similar clothes and had dark skin from the sun. The Crusaders couldn't tell the difference. But the crusading Latins won the day and were now in charge of Jerusalem.'

'Pope Urban died before the news of the victory could reach him. The victors then set about dividing Palestine into states, Jerusalem, Edessa, Antioch and Tripol, putting the most senior dukes and barons in charge of the various areas. The land was now called Outremer meaning "Over the sea." As most of these so called leaders were still quarreling with each other and as they all had quite sizable armies, in fact at first, they spent so much time fighting amongst themselves that they really had little time or inclination to fight any invaders or enemies.'

'A King of Jerusalem was finally appointed and over the next hundred years life settled down. Generations of young men, knights with nothing much to do, would go to Outremer, join the army of a king, lord or baron helping to defend the land against invaders or anyone who dared to annoy the Latin Franks, as they became known to the local people.'

'Some of the barons had made friends with their

Arab neighbours, and lived in peace. But some of the Arab leaders were not about to forgive the Latins for the Jerusalem bloodshed of 1099 and constantly attacked them. There was an awful lot of quarrelling and killing.'

'And so we come forward to the 1170s and although the Franks had been ruling Outremer since 1099, there had been little peace and even less stability across the region. The Frankish leaders still quarreled amongst themselves; the Arab nations also quarreled with each other; and of course Franks and Arabs constantly battled with each other. They all believed the others had no right to be there anyway. The local tribes who were there in the first place still considered the Latins as invaders. But many Franks had been born in Outremer being the descendants of those first Crusaders and, knowing nothing of their ancestral homes in Europe, felt they had EVERY right to be there. It was a bit of a mess all round really.'

'There were also people on both sides who firmly believed that the country was big enough for all nationalities and all could live in peace.'

'However it was not to be,' said Chris shuffling his papers. 'for in 1187 the Franks were finally driven out of Jerusalem and most of Outremer after a tremendous battle. It was a savage massacre in which, having read Guy's story, I realised he was involved. But being a young man of 16 or 17 at the time and later, as he wrote his memoirs, he would hardly have known then that his battle would be so famous or infamous.' Chris chuckled to himself.

'Neither would he have known of the years of bickering and strife that led up to those awful days of July 3rd and 4th 1187, which became known as the Battle of Hattin.

77

History tells us of the years before that massacre and of the star players who were probably the main causes of this final battle. Some were good caring men, some were unbelievably stupid but some were just downright evil. It's hard to believe what some of these mad men did in those years from 1150 onwards.'

'Count Raymond of Tiberias and Tripoli was a good sensible General. He had been born in Outremer, had many Arab friends and spoke several Arab languages and as the king's cousin he was the most senior member of the nobility.'

'He firmly believed that all could live in peace and despite being a mighty general of a huge army he was thoroughly sick of the constant fighting and killing. Because of this he was called a traitor and coward by some of his more militant neighbours and warmongering generals.'

'When the young King of Jerusalem died suddenly, as the most senior noble, Raymond should have been crowned king but his many enemies secretly crowned the dead king's sister and her wimpish husband, Guido, King and Queen of Jerusalem. Count Raymond was furious and together with many of his friends refused to accept this upstart Guido as king. The rift between the Frankish barons almost caused a civil war. Saladin, the famous leader of the combined Arab nations, was delighted. If these Latin Franks were to go to war with each other, tear each other to pieces and wipe each other out, it would save him a job.'

'Saladin, was a general and commander of a huge Arab army. He had spent many years trying to persuade the many, many nationalities of Seljuks, the Kurdish nations,

Egyptians, Mamelukes, Assassins and the many small tribes from across Asia Minor, all speaking different languages, to work together as one mighty army to push the Latin Franks out of Outremer. In the year 1183 he finally persuaded his countrymen that ridding their lands of the foreigners was a good idea and over the next four years he set about training them to fight as one army, second to none in size and force. All fighting together was a new experience for them as they usually battled with each other.'

'Saladin, although a brave warrior and soldier and sometimes even a ruthless killer, could be a reasonable, kindly and honest man. He demanded loyalty and hated cheats and liars and above all injustice. He was also tired of the constant warring and fighting and wanted the whole mess to be over. He had a few Frankish friends, men he considered honourable, Count Raymond being one of them, but he also had a few pet hates. The top of his most wanted list was Gerard de Ridford.'

'Gerard de Ridford was Grand Master of the Knights Templar. He was an irritable, bad tempered and aggressive man and although a brave knight and general he was hasty and headstrong. He was said to be reckless, incompetent and arrogant. In fact it's a puzzlement how he got the job of Grand Master at all. One of the most foolish things he did was after there had been a terrible drought over the whole land. There was not enough water for men or animals and a truce was agreed between Saladin, Count Raymond and the King that there should be no more warring and fighting until the land had recovered. Saladin's son had asked permission of Count Raymond to cross the Frankish lands with a battalion

Caravan

of his troops as a reconnaissance and training exercise. Although Raymond knew it was probably a spying trip, he could hardly refuse because of the truce.'

'De Ridford was furious when he heard of it and calling Raymond every kind of fool, hastily gathered about 200 of his Knights Templar and set off at a gallop to show these enemy spies who was master. To his horror, what he found was an army of some 7000 highly trained Turkish cavalry quietly trotting to Acre. Unable to admit his foolishness and quite unable to back off he ordered his knights to attack! They had to obey of course. It was a massacre. Every Templar except three were killed and then beheaded. De Ridford escaped - one of the three.'

'The newly crowned King Guido of Jerusalem, who was a bit of a wimp and not the Knights' Templar or the army's idea of a warrior leader, was furious with de Ridford because had broken the truce with Saladin of whom he was terrified.'

'The job of being King had been forced upon him by his wife who had been determined to be crowned Queen after her brother died. He was no fighting man, nobody's idea of a warrior and preferred a peaceful life with his books. Gerard de Ridford called him a coward but then Gerard de Ridford called everyone a coward! King Guido had been trained as a knight but going off to war was not his idea of a day out. However, as king, he had to lead his army and as we shall see later, shaped up fairly well as he lead his troops into battle.'

'Another famous young man was Raynald de Chatillan. He was the youngest son of a wealthy aristocratic French family who had been taught all the skills of knighthood but had no land, titles or money in France. His elder brother had taken the lot. As a penniless knight he decided to go to Outremer to seek his fortune and when King Louis Vll of France set off with his army in 1147 Raynald tagged along.'

'He was a brave knight and soldier and did a good job fighting alongside King Louis and the other crusading knights but somewhere inside he was a very wicked, greedy young man. It was a sad day for Outremer when he decided to stay behind when his king went back to France. He joined the King of Jerusalem's army and made many friends amongst the Knights Templar who thought him a fine brave soldier which of course he was, and a really good chap which he was not!'

'In a battle to free Antioch he fought so bravely alongside the King and the Knights Templar that the Princess Constance of Antioch fell in love with him and decided she would marry this young brave handsome French knight. 'Yippee!' said Raynald who now had riches, wealth, a castle and a princess for a wife, but best of all he was now the Prince of Antioch with his own army! He had made his fortune.'

'But he was greedy wanting always more power and more wealth. In 1160 he heard that groups of herdsmen moved their animals off the cold mountains to spend the winter on the warmer valleys of the river Euphrates. He cast his greedy eyes over this huge number of animals and realising the herdsmen and shepherds were unarmed he gathered his army of knights and attacked them stealing their animals and scattering the herdsmen.'

'He set off home delighted with himself driving the animals ahead of him. However somebody had ridden away for help and Raynald got the shock of his life when he met an army of cavalry sent to rescue the shepherds. Reynald was thrown into prison and stayed there for 16 years.'

'When he came out in 1176 his wife was dead and he was no longer a Prince. Once again he had no money and nowhere to live so he began to look around for a new wealthy wife. He found one! She was a very rich lady who owned not one but two castles and he then became known as the Lord of Kerak. Parts of Kerak Castle are still there today.'

'During his years in jail he had learned to speak both Turkish and Arabic and was now able to pay Arab spies to bring him information about Saladin and what he was doing and the positions of wealthy trading caravans for him to plunder.'

'In 1186 there was another truce between Saladin and Count Raymond. Peace reigned. People began to trade again and huge caravans travelled between Egypt and Mecca loaded with precious silks, spices and salt. This was all too much for Reynald. The sight of these rich caravans passing the windows of his castle was more than his greedy heart could bare. So, truce or no truce - guess what -?'

'He raided one of them?' asked Guy.

'Afraid he did - breaking the truce again of course. Silly man. He again had gathered his troops together and attacked a large caravan of merchants and their families stealing all their riches and animals and he threw everyone into his dungeons at Kerak. Historians tell us that a relative of Saladin, possibly his sister or his aunt, was traveling with that caravan.'

'Saladin appealed to King Guido for the release of the merchants and the return of their goods. But Reynald refused the King's demands.'

'Saladin was furious. He said that if he ever caught Reynald he would kill him with his bare hands and said he had no choice but to go to war with these Franks and push them out of the his land altogether. And so having gathered all his forces together he was ready for war.'

'Who were the Knights Templar?' I asked.

'They were an elite army of men who were both knights and monks. They protected people travelling to Outremer from bandits who were often waiting to rob, kill and even sell the travellers to slave traders. They called themselves Knights of the Temple of Jerusalem - Knights Templar for short. Slowly, as their brotherhood got bigger, they became a highly trained band of fighting men helping the king and the barons to protect Outremer against their enemies.

'To qualify as a Knight Templar a young man must be a son of a noble, rich aristocratic family and a qualified knight. Once accepted into the Order he must leave his family and live within the brotherhood of monks and abide by the very strict rules set down for them. As monks they could never marry. They were allowed no personal possessions except their clothes, armour, weapons and horses and must give absolute unquestioning obedience to the Grand Master who, in 1187 was this fellow Gerard de Ridford. They were an army of hundreds, feared by their enemies. They did not fight as individuals but as a solid body of men and because they believed that they were doing God's work they had no fear of personal injury or death. The Brotherhood never paid ransom to Saladin for any of the Knights Templar whom he held prisoner. Any member of the order captured by Saladin was executed at once, if not sooner, as they were incidentally very good at escaping captivity. Saladin hated them in their white tabards with a red cross.'

'There was incidentally another army of knight monks in Outremer at that time. Like the Templars, they were a brotherhood who had been formed originally to provide wayside food and lodging for travellers and also hospital care for the sick and wounded. They were the Order of St John of the Hospital of Jerusalem and became known as the Hospitallers. They wore a black tunic with a white cross. Saladin hated them too.'

'And so we now go on to July 1187 and the massacre at Hattin, Saladin with his great army poised ready to go, the King of Jerusalem mustering his troops.

CHAPTER 10

THE BATTLE OF HATTIN

'The Battle of Hattin was fought on the 3rd of July 1187. Historians differ slightly in their accounts so we must take an overall picture. Later we will read Guy's story, which I have here on the table, because of course he was there!' Chris continued.

'King Guido was informed by his spies that Saladin had gathered the biggest army that he'd ever commanded for his holy war. The king called a meeting of all his generals at Jerusalem. The meeting included Raynald de Chatillan, whose actions had so upset Saladin. Gerard de Ridford (the maniac who during the truce had ordered the attack on 7000 Arab cavalry with only about 200 Knights Templar - and lost.) was also invited together with all the Dukes, Barons and leaders of the Outremer states and Count Raymond, still the most senior Lord and General under the King.'

'At the meeting Raymond said that the army must be based where there was shade from the summer heat and water for both men and animals. Then, the Franks, having got such a prime position, could sit and wait. Such a place was Sephoria. Once they were ensconced, Saladin's army would probably go home as no army could fight without water. And so over the next days the armies under their Generals were mustered and set off to Sephoria. By July 2nd all had arrived near Sephoria and made camp. They just had to dig in and wait.'

'The King had called every man who could fight, to his side. There were thousands of men speaking many languages and dialects. Greeks and Syrians and Latin Franks from all over Outremer were gathered, the biggest army ever known up to that time.'

'Then a terrible thing happened. A messenger came from Raymond's wife in Tiberias about 20 miles away. A part of Saladin's army had attacked Raymond's lands around Tiberias, had taken the city and were now besieging his castle where his wife and garrison were defending themselves. A very clever move by Saladin knowing that Raymond and his sons were all with the King at Sephoria. Some said "We must go and save Tiberias." But Count Raymond said "No! This is a Saladin trick to get us to move from our safe haven. Anyway," he said, "Tiberias is my land and is probably lost to Saladin." It was his wife in the castle and he felt sure he could ransom her afterwards; Saladin was always very chivalrous to women anyway and Raymond was sure she would not be harmed. So it was agreed that they stay where they were.'

'However during the night Gerard de Ridford and Raynald de Chatillan went to the King's tent to persuaded him to go and save Tiberias. Because de Ridford hated Count Raymond, probably jealous of his rank and position, he was determined to overrule anything Raymond said. He convinced the King that the Count was a traitorous coward and he was probably in league with Saladin, which incidentally was totally untrue. De Ridford managed to persuade the King that Raymond's plans were rubbish. And so the King, not wishing to be called a coward, finally relented and gave orders to

March to Tiberias in the morning. The men were called at dawn and word was passed through the camp that the King had changed his mind.'

'To advance across the waterless plain to get to Tiberias was suicide as the particularly stupid King had refused to bring any water wagons for the troops. He had said that each man must carry his own water supply. How he had hoped to water the horses I can't imagine, although some pack animals did carry water skins.

'The Barons, Knights, Generals and Knights Templar were furious. Some demanded of the King "Why?" as Tiberias was already lost. We believe the King felt a little stupid but had hated the thought of being called a coward by de Ridford.'

'Saladin was encamped in the hills overlooking the planned march. Everyone knew that there would not be enough water, but the King said "Go!" and everyone had to obey. Saladin's spies watched them breaking camp at dawn and setting off towards Tiberias. Saladin was delighted. His trap had worked.'

'As this mass of men marched, Saladin's cavalry galloped round the edges of the columns, firing arrows into them and then swiftly galloping off. As the day wore on the sun got higher and the heat became intense. Travelling in armour under the hot sun soaked with sweat, they desperately needed water as they trudged through those bleak dusty hills with no shade. By mid-morning they had been marching six hours.'

'Raymond still leading the vanguard said they must go faster but the rearguard could not keep up. The exhausted foot soldiers could not go any faster. By midday most of their water had gone. They had all hoped to stop at a stream of water at Mount Turan but the King stupidly said that they must march on.'

'As the day wore on Raymond wanted to press on to Tiberias but the rearguard led by Gerard de Ridford now several miles behind, said no and called to the King to halt. Raymond was furious. He had decided that they must try to get to the springs at Hattin where there was water and all could rest but a rider came from the King saying that they must halt here in the Lubian waterless plain.'

'Saladin meantime, realising Raymond's plan, sent a couple of divisions ahead to block the road leading to the water springs of Hattin. Twin hills known as the Horns of Hattin fringed the plain where the Franks halted. A road dropped down to the Sea of Galilea beyond the hills and Raymond and the barons wanted to force their way through to the waters of the great lake but the path was blocked by Saladin's Seljuk division. The rearguard was still far behind, still trying to catch up with the column, still being constantly attacked by the enemy archers. When the whole army was finally gathered some of the desperately thirsty foot soldiers went to find a well up on the slope but found it dry and they were killed by enemy scouts. And so with no water they settled down for the night; they were now at least cool.'

'There was little peace however. Saladin's army kept up a constant horrendous noise, yelling, blowing trumpets, banging drums while small contingents galloped round firing arrows at the men.'

'Saladin then had another bright idea. To add to the Frank's misery he set the scrub and dry grass on fire all along the hillside. The breeze took the smoke across the

Frankish camp and the army spent a miserable night unable to sleep, coughing.'

'During the night Saladin brought in droves of camels carrying water skins for his troops and dromedaries loaded with more arrows for the coming battle. Then under cover of darkness and smoke he moved his huge army to encircle the Franks along the hill tops. At first light the Franks found themselves totally surrounded by the enemy. A mass of infantry tried to break through the enemy lines and dash down the other side of the hill to the fresh clear water of the lake but they were all cut to pieces or taken prisoner by Saladin's army. King Guido nevertheless, ordered the troops to march on as they had done the day before, Raymond at the front, the King himself and his knights in the middle and the Knights Templar and their sergeants bringing up the rear.'

'Suddenly, at a sign from Saladin, the battle began, his screaming, yelling troops charged into the Frankish army from all sides. Slashing at them with their scimitars and swords, wave upon wave of foot soldiers and cavalry crashed their way down the hillside as thousands of arrows rained down from the skilful mounted archers. One historian said "The sky was so black with arrows that they blotted out the sun."'

'The Frankish army struggled on but a frightful rout followed. Raymond and a group of knights broke through the enemy lines leading a charge but Saladin's troops closed in behind them and they couldn't get back to the main battle. Saladin's General then let them gallop away. Raymond later was accused of desertion by the King and Saladin's General was in trouble for letting them get away!'

'This left the infantry without some of its cavalry protection. The Latins charged and charged again at Saladin's forces but by now many of the knights' horses were dead, killed by the arrows of the enemy archers whose job it was to kill the horses, bringing the knights to the ground. A knight on horseback was a terrifying fighting machine but on foot, carrying all that weight of armour, his sword and his shield, he could hardly walk let alone fight. Some knights, boiling inside their armour, exhausted from lack of water and sleep (having coughed all night) just collapsed and were cut to pieces or taken prisoner to be killed or ransomed later. Many foot soldiers just surrendered. Knights Templar and Hospitaller were shown no mercy and any that survived were beheaded next day.'

'The Franks had lost the battle; it had been a massacre. Many of Saladin's soldiers were dead too of course but the Frankish army had been almost wiped out or taken prisoner. The King had mustered every fighting man for this battle from all over Outremer which left nobody defending it. It was said that only two knights remained in Jerusalem. Heat, exhaustion and thirst had not helped the Franks but Saladin had been very clever and because of a couple of hotheaded warmongering knights, de Ridford's and Raynald's bad advice, the King had fallen right into his trap. Some knights and barons were made prisoner and ransomed back to their families but many hundreds, together with their horses, lay dead on the hillside and the plain below.'

'After the battle King Guido and Reynald de Chatillan, our old friend, were amongst the captured and taken to Saladin's tent shaking with fear, filthy dirty and both still dying of thirst. Saladin, as I have explained before, was an honourable man, handed the King a drink of iced water, some say rose water, which the King drank gratefully. He then handed the bowl to Reynald. Saladin was angry and said that the King must remember that he, Saladin, had not given Reynald water to drink. It is an Arabic custom that when one is invited into an Arabic house or in this case a tent, and is offered food or drink, one is then safe within.'

'Saladin then began to tell Reynald just what he thought of him, breaking truces, attacking unarmed shepherds and merchants, stealing, lying and betraying trusts. Reynald who could speak arabic became very angry and was very rude to Saladin. Saladin I guess had heard enough. He took his sword and with one mighty swipe, some say, sliced off Reynald's head. Others say he sliced down through his shoulder taking off his arm; the guards then dragged him outside and finished him off.'

I looked at Guy. We were both horrified.

Crusader Castle of Kerak
Now in Jordan

'You mean he actually swiped off his head in one go?'

'So we are told.' said Uncle Chris.

I didn't say a word but I remember thinking what a terrible mess there must have been on the floor of Saladin's tent.

Chris continued. 'After the battle all the captured Templars and Hospitallers together with their sergeants were put to death. Only one man was spared - their Grand Master - Gerard de Ridford. Many senior knights and barons were ransomed back to their families giving Saladin a fortune in gold. Count Raymond had got away during the battle you remember and Saladin did allow his wife to leave their castle at Tiberias with all her ladies and all her household goods. She probably rejoined her husband.'

Guy and I sat silent for a while; that had been quite a story. I felt sorry for the poor horses. Chris put his notes together and returned his books to the old box. 'I really think it's your supper time.' he said looking at the clock on the mantelpiece. 'Your Mother said 6.30, Guy, and it's now a quarter to seven - better run. If it's wet again tomorrow and you've nothing better to do, come round and I'll tell you Guy's story - around 3 o'clock again?'

The heavy rain of the afternoon had stopped and the clouds were breaking up showing bits of blue sky. The grass was wet as we trudged back to the house but everything felt clean and washed after the storms.

The Mystery of a Lost Sword and Scimitar

CHAPTER 11

GUY

It was Monday and we had agreed to meet Chris in the big library in Guy's house, as the master copy of Chris' book was kept there.

'I've been looking at the original narrative of Guy's time in Outremer written by this Friar Pierre as Guy dictated.' Chris explained. 'You'll hear more of Friar Pierre later. But how it was ever translated into English from Pierre's original in the 1600s I'll never know. However I shall read you my translation of Guy's tale as if he was telling it, just as Pierre wrote it.' Chris opened his folder and started to read.

'My name is Guido de Ville. I shall be 20 years old on July 10th. The year is now 1190 and here we begin.'

'When I was 9 years old I went to stay with my uncle, my mother's brother, in France, to learn the skills of knighthood. I had already had some schooling in my own language, Norman-French, and the local Anglo-Saxon. In France at my Uncle's castle I would be taught to be a knight, to use a sword, a lance, a battle axe, how to carry a shield on horseback. I would learn about armour and how to wear it. There were other boys at the castle, sons of Dukes and noblemen all learning the art of knighthood. We boys would all begin as pages; we may have to serve at table and do menial tasks in the kitchens. We had to care for and feed the master's horses and dogs and even polish the Lord's armour. If we had pleased our Lord and

Master, at 12 years we became squires but all the time still learning the skills of war, weapons and knighthood.'

'When I was 16 years old my Mother's nephew, cousin William, decided to become a Knight Templar and go to Outremer. He was 20 and had been made a knight two years ago. He said he was bored living in the castle and that he wanted to go and join an army and fight like a soldier. His parents were horrified; to be a Knight Templar he must give everything he owned, which wasn't much as he was the youngest son in the family, to the order of the Knights Templar. He would be allowed his horses, his uniform and his weapons. He would not be allowed to marry or have any contact with his mother or sister as he was joining the order of warrior monks. The family tried to discourage him but he was determined to go and what was more, he offered to take me along with him. I was thrilled and so excited.'

'I and my cousin came home to England to get my father's permission. Father was delighted with the idea but mother was not too happy about it. She felt I was still too young. It was decided however, despite his mother's protests, that I should go with William to Outremer for perhaps a couple of years. Things were fairly peaceful there after all, they thought!'

'As we said our farewells my father gave me a sword, which had belonged to my grandfather, and a horse. My mother gave me a pouch, to be worn round my waist. It contained a lock of her hair, a leather flask made to contain water and a small container of her special ointment. This she made herself from honey and various plants and moulds, used for healing wounds. She said it might help if I was wounded.'

Chris said 'I don't know how Guy and his cousin's party got to Jerusalem except that they must have gone by land as it took 4 months to get there. He tells us nothing of the journey. The next time we hear of him he is in Jerusalem in the barracks set aside for Sergeants attached to the Knights Templar, but Guy continues.'

'When we arrived in the Knights' Templar camp in Jerusalem my cousin left me to register in the barracks set aside for Sergeants away from the Knights Templar. The Sergeants were a powerful army within the Knights Templar force. They fought alongside the Knights Templar in battle, cared for the horses and the knight's armour. In some cases the older sergeants were very experienced campaigners, more so than some of the young Knights Templar, and highly intelligent. Sadly, because they were low born probably of the peasant classes, they could never become Knights.'

'During those first few months I hated it. Life there was not as I had expected. I was home sick, disliked the strange food, strange climate and army life. I just wanted to go home.'

'It was a big camp of about 200 sergeants. We, the youngsters, had all the dirty jobs to do - mucking out the stables and looking after the horses. We also had to clean and care for the Knights' Templar armour. We did, however, have some servants, captured in battle, who cooked our meals and cleaned the barracks.'

'During the day the weather was hot but always cold at night. We were glad of our cloaks as we only had one blanket each. There was always a shortage of water. We didn't wash much as water was needed for drinking for both men and horses. We young sergeants in the barracks slept on a hard stone floor on sacks filled with straw. A light was always kept burning at night. We were fed meat twice a day, as were the Templars, because we had to be fit and strong for fighting the wars. As sergeants we all wore black or brown uniforms, a jerkin and long breeches with a black cloak.'

'There was much talk around the campfires at night of wars and fighting. The older sergeants, some of whom had been with the Knights Templar for many years and had fought lots of battles and survived, also talked about the war which was surely to come. The Lord of Kerak, Raynald de Chatillan, had broken another truce with Lord Saladin; so had our Grand Master, Lord de Ridford. The men said there would surely be a battle. Anyway, Saladin hated the Knights Templar. We young ones were all a bit frightened. Spies had told the King that Saladin had gathered a great army together a few miles away over the River Jordan. One sergeant said "They'll drive us all out of Outremer. You mark my words!" Others called him an old woman and said we were a far better army than Saladin's lot and we'd beat them every time.'

'In early June the King called all the Lords to meet him here at Jerusalem. We were told that they were planning the great battle. Over the next weeks we trained for it. I was very frightened and wished I could be at home with my parents. We prepared and packed all the armour; our archers cleaned and packed hundreds of bows and arrows made by our blacksmiths. Our cooks made and dried bread and meat. There was great excitement and activity in the camp.'

'On the 29th of June we set off, walking towards a place called Sephoria. We would join all the other

Knights Templar from all over Outremer under our Grand Master. The King was going to do battle with Saladin and every man who could fight was required. All the Lords and Barons with their Knights would be gathered there. It took us two days to get to a place near Sephoria. Hundreds of men were already encamped when we got there. Every army under their leader had its own flag.'

'It was a magnificent sight - all those colours - and all those standards and flags fluttering in the wind. I now felt so proud and brave being part of this vast company. Surely nothing could stop us winning. We, the sergeants, had all been issued with thick leather jerkins which were said to protect us from arrows but they were very heavy and hot. Some of the senior sergeants were mounted and even wore chain mail.'

'Count Raymond, the most senior Knight under the King, had said "We must all get to Sephoria." He would lead the column with his own knights and his sons. In the centre rode the King and the Bishops, protected by his knights and his infantry. Then came all the other Barons with their armies. In the rearguard came the Knights Templar, with their white surcoats and red crosses, and us together with more foot soldiers. Hundreds of foot soldiers marched all round the edges of the columns as they had to help protect the horses with their bodies. These men wore thick leather armour which the enemy arrows, hopefully, could not penetrate. Some of the horses wore leather skirts to protect them but they hated wearing them; they made them too hot.'

'We each carried a flask of water and some of the pack animals carried heavy goatskins filled with water for the horses. The older sergeants complained that there was not enough but the stupid King refused to take the water wagons. We, the young sergeants, were to march in the middle of the rearguard forces. Some of the foot soldiers right at the end of the column would be forced to march backwards for miles protecting us from the Saracen archers and lancers.'

'At a signal Count Raymond started and slowly everybody began to move off. We marched all day 'til we came to a very green valley, the place called Sephoria. There was plenty of water and our men said we would be safe there. But the place was already seething with armies from all over Outremer, all speaking different languages that I couldn't understand. The King's tent was guarded by a troop of his special soldiers all wearing the King's colours. Most of the knights were there on this vast field, grouped around their Lord or Baron when we, the rearguard, got there.

Our Knights Templar and sergeants were complaining that all the best camp spots had already gone. I and four of my friends, young sergeants like me, found ourselves a corner close to the others of our barracks and made ourselves a fire. We were given bread which our cooks had brought with them. It was very hard and dry but we were so hungry by then. We also got some dried meat and there was plenty of water. We sergeants all had to help feed and water the horses whilst our Knights Templar sat in groups round fires.'

'My cousin came over to see me and told us that the King intended to stay here at this spot. Saladin would not attack us here as to reach us he and his army had to march across a stretch of parched waterless land which was too far to go without water. He would probably go home. We were glad as we sat round our little fire. None of us would have admitted that we were afraid but I know that we were all pleased that there would be no battle. We could all use a sword but we had never had to fight for our lives. I still carried grandfather's sword. I wondered what he would have thought of me.'

'As the sun went down it began to get colder and we settled down for the night. It was a good sight seeing all those hundreds of campfires twinkling in the darkness. The stars over our heads were very bright in a clear sky. Somewhere not far away a man began to sing and everybody stopped talking to listen. There was complete silence except for this marvelous man's voice. It sounded a sad song sung in a language which I didn't understand. Suddenly I wanted to be at home safe, sitting on the floor beside a roaring fire with my parents and my dog. Good job my mother couldn't see me now.'

'I wrapped myself in my cloak and must have fallen asleep for suddenly I was startled by men standing up and voices shouting 'What is it? What's going on?' We five now all awake stood up too, trying to see what the trouble was. There was something going on over by the King's tent. As a couple of our Knights Templar wandered over to see what was wrong somebody said 'Perhaps somebody has stuck a knife in the King!' Another voice said 'Hope so!' and they all laughed. The King was not popular with the men.'

'By now our Grand Master, Lord de Ridford, had been wakened and was making his way over to the King's tent with more of our Knights Templar. We all waited. Every soldier was awake by now. It was cold; we built up the fires. All sorts of stories were passed around. The

King was dead; the Count Raymond had been poisoned; somebody had stolen the wagon of arrows. We waited by our fires for answers.'

'Eventually our Knights Templar returned and told us that the Lord Saladin had attacked and captured Tiberias, the land owned by Count Raymond, and was besieging his castle where the Count's wife and her guards were trying to defend themselves. Some said that the King's army should go and rescue her but Raymond had said no, this was one of Saladin's tricks to get us to move from this safe place to somewhere towards Tiberias where his army could attack us. Anyway, one chap said, there was only one small spring between here and Tiberias. We would all die of thirst.'

'The King had agreed with Raymond and so we all went back to sleep. I woke again - and again there was shouting - men running about - it seemed for no reason at all that I could see - it was still dark - what now? "The stupid King has changed his mind." a senior sergeant told us. "We have to go and save Tiberias. Get up! Fill your water bottles from the stream and get the horses saddled. Some of you help the knights into their armour."'

'"Any chance of some food, Sergeant?"one of my friends asked. He was always hungry. "No time for food, boy!" the sergeant answered. "We march at dawn!" The Knights Templar were furious, all grumbling that they had to go and save Tiberias which they considered a lost cause. We would be too late.'

'My cousin came and advised us to get as much water as we could carry - fill anything that would hold water. We rushed around and found some empty wineskins the men had emptied the night before. We filled them with water. We would have to cross a place called Lubiya where there was no water at all. We were told later that the Lords de Ridford and de Chatillan had gone to the King's tent in secret during the night and had persuaded him to change his mind and go and save Count Raymond's wife and castle.'

'By the time the sun came up we were all ready to move off. Hundreds of men, each in their national groups, were waiting for Count Raymond, the leader, to mount his horse. One sergeant, an old soldier, said that they don't know what they're doing and that we should all stay here where we were safe.'

'Setting off, we with the Knights Templar, were again at the rear but now we also had foot soldiers marching with us.'

'We had marched a long time. The sun was hot as it slowly climbed up overhead. The sweat was running down my back under my jerkin. Leaving the green valley far behind, the ground was dry and dusty. We at the back were forced to march through all the dust churned up by those thousands of men and horses in the front. The horses were very distressed by it, we tried to cover their noses with wet cloths but they didn't like that either. Our knights were angry. They said we were too slow.'

'Towards midday most of us had run out of water. Suddenly somebody shouted "Saracens!" and a hail of arrows flew over into our midst. Some of our men were screaming. One Knight Templar shouted to us to tighten ranks and we all closed into a tight bunch. This attack was only the beginning. The enemy archers, hundreds of them, continued all day dashing in towards us firing arrows and then riding off on their fast little horses.

"Firing arrows and then riding off
on their fast little horses."

Some of our knights gave chase. We just kept marching on towards Tiberias. Our archers were trying to protect us but the enemy was so very fast and very accurate.'

'The whole army now had to travel more slowly. The knights on horseback were forced to ride as slowly as the slowest foot soldier and by late day we were all very slow. There was no water left. The day wore on; the heat was cruel. The horses were desperate for water and knights were boiling inside their armour. Some were even throwing their armour off and all the time the enemy archers continued their attack. They aimed for the horses killing many of them and so left their knights stumbling around in full armour on foot.'

'Some of the infantry had tried to get up and over the hillside and down the other side to a great lake of fresh water but had all been killed by the enemy.'

'Everybody was grumbling. "I bet the King has water!" said a voice. "Aye, and his horse!" said another.'

'A messenger rode back to our master. The king did not intend to stop for water at a place called Cresson, so we were to go on to the springs at Hattin. Somebody said that Count Raymond at the front was quite close to these springs and wanted to press on but we at the back were miles away. Then we were told that the Lord Saladin had sent a troop of his soldiers to block the pass leading to Hattin and the water. We all had to march on to a dusty dry valley surrounded by hillsides and camp for the night.'

'Camped on that hillside, we spent an awful night. The enemy seemed to be all around us and kept up the most awful noise of drums and rattles and screaming. Then they set fire to the dry field grass all around us. The wind blew the smoke across and we were choking. They also continued to fire hundreds of arrows into our midst. We were forced to try to sleep holding leather jerkins over our heads.'

'As the dawn came up we set off to march onward but we saw that the enemy had completely surrounded us and suddenly they attacked from all sides at once. Their screaming cavalry with slashing swords broke through our ranks while arrows landed among us. We still had no water and had had little or no sleep. Some of our older sergeants gathered us young ones together on to the hillside to protect us. But it was no use - they were all cut down by the swords and scimitars of the mounted enemy. The last thing I remember was running down the hillside to the flat ground below. We were slashing from side to side with our swords at their foot soldiers. Suddenly I must have been knocked to the ground. I remember a terrible pain at the back of my head. Everything suddenly seemed to go slow. There was a ringing in my ears and this terrible pain. The ground was coming up to meet me.'

CHAPTER 12

ALIVE!

'When I opened my eyes it was getting dark. I was lying face down on the ground. I tried to lift my head but the pain at the back of my head and neck was terrible. I couldn't move. Everything was quiet. I also had an awful pain in the bones of my chest but then I realised I was lying on my sword; lucky I hadn't sliced myself in half!

'I tried to remember what had happened and slowly the awful memories came back. All the noise and all the screaming of men and wounded horses. I began to shiver. I was so cold. Then I remembered I was still thirsty. I rolled over on to my back, I must sit up but each time I tried the whole world went round and round. I felt sick and the pain in my head was awful. I closed my eyes and forced myself to sit up hanging on to my knees until the spinning stopped.'

'I finally managed to open my eyes and what a terrible sight I saw. All around me and as far as I could see in all directions everything was dead! Men, thousands of men - Arabs - Saracens - Latins and horses - all dead. All so still. I wondered who had won the battle. In the far distance walking away from me were a group of men in Arab dress with a number of carts drawn by horses. They seemed to be picking things up off the ground and throwing them into the wagons. I realised that they were gathering up weapons, armour, arrows perhaps and anything they could sell. They had passed me over thinking I was dead. I knew they must not see me but I had to get up and try to find some water. We had been told that the soldiers of Saladin had plenty of water so I staggered about looking for a dead enemy who might still have a water bottle on his belt. I found two and drank one fastening the other to my belt. I sat down again wondering what to do. Then - a sound - a rustling. Grabbing my sword I looked about me - nothing - but there it was again. Something was moving quite near me. I heard the rustling again and then I saw a hand move among a pile of clothing. Somebody was alive. I crawled over to him. His eyes were open and he was trying to say something. "Ahb - Ahb!" He was an Arab. Water! He wanted water! I gave him a drink and he gulped it down, as thirsty as I had been.'

'He still wore what had been a rich yellow silk tabard over his uniform but like me he was very dirty. He was young, perhaps younger than me but he looked very pale. We were enemies; Lord de Ridford, our Grand Master, would have called him a barbarian and would probably have killed him. I had seen enough killing to last me all my life and that field didn't need any more dead bodies. I looked at his white face. He seemed to be asleep, dying perhaps or wounded. His arms seemed good but then I looked at his legs. One was uninjured but a sword had sliced the other. The wound was a deep cut and there was a lot of blood on the ground but it seemed to have stopped bleeding. He was coming round. He groaned, opened his eyes and looked at me. "Ahb!" he said and smiled.'

'It was almost dark now. We should get off this field. Somebody might come back and kill one or both of us. Standing up I tried to get him to his feet. He tried to help himself but cried out in pain. His leg was bleeding again. I hoped nobody had heard him. We were both shivering.

I pointed to the wide gash across the top of his leg. I said "Bad?" He nodded then suddenly I remembered my mother's ointment.

I took out the little leather box. Taking off the lid, its familiar smell reminded me of home and watching my mother mixing what she called her magic potion. Let's hope its magic would work on his leg. I knew men could lose a leg or even die from wounds half as bad as this. I spread the ointment all round the edge of the gash and hoped some would run down into the wound. I needed something to bind the leg. He sensed what I needed and struggled out of his silk tabard. We tore it in half and I wrapped it round his leg as tight as I could bringing the awful wound together. He smiled, nodded; it must have been very painful.'

'I finally got him to stand up but he couldn't put any weight on his leg. I gave him my sword to use as a crutch and put his other arm over my shoulder. My head was throbbing. I felt sick and dizzy but we had to get off this field of bodies. We struggled up the hillside it seemed for ages. At last we managed to find a shelter between two huge rock boulders. I could go no further. We sat huddled together and I wrapped us both in my cloak.'

'I woke as the daylight began to light up the sky. My head still hurt but the dizziness had gone. I looked at my companion. He was still asleep. His face was white. I thought again that he was dead but then he opened his eyes and looked at me. "Ahb! Ahb!" he whispered (Water). There was not much left but I handed it to him. He shook it – took a great gulp – then handed it back. "Shoma! " he smiled (You). I drank what was left.'

'He leaned back against the rock with a great sigh

and said "Frank?" I nodded. The Arabs called all us all Franks. Then he smiled again and said "I - am - Davoud. What - is - your - name?"' The shock of hearing him speak my language must have shown on my face because he laughed and then we were both laughing. He was not very fluent and he spoke very slowly to make me understand but spoke enough of my Norman-French to explain who he was.'

'His father was a merchant and hated these constant wars with the Latin Franks and said that the world needed trade not war. They lived in Damascus but came originally from Iran. He had not wanted Davoud to go to the battle but, like me, he had joined his father's brother who was an officer in one of Saladin's Egyptian regiments. Fighting and killing the infidel - us - had seemed like a good idea at the time.'

'Talking was hard work for him. We were both very weak and had no food and no water. He said that there was water, little springs farther up the hillside. He also said that if I go back to the battlefield I might find some food in the bags carried by Saladin's soldiers. The fact that any of Saladin's soldiers I might find there would have been dead for a day, together with everything else on that battlefield, and the thought of going back there at all even for food and water, was not my idea of a party. But we needed food and water desperately; also I may find a few cloaks from the English knights to keep us warm if those people with carts had left anything. We were in a fairly safe place sheltered by these boulders so I left Davoud and set off back down the hill.'

'The battlefield was a terrible sight. Yesterday had seemed bad enough as we had struggled away in the fading light but today in the sunshine it was a thousand times worse. I sat down and thought, "How stupid! All these men and horses killed, why and for what?"'

'I carefully picked my way across the hillside and field. I found a number of bags on the bodies of Arabs and Saracens. Hard bread, strips of dried meat and lumps of a sweet cake. I stuffed it all into one bag. I gathered as many water skins as I could carry, then grabbed four knight's cloaks and hurried back to the safety of our rocks.'

'Davoud was pleased to see me and so it was over the next four days we stayed hidden amongst the rocks and boulders. Davoud found walking very difficult and painful and we were afraid to stray far from our hideout as we were both in danger from each other's troops. If we had been caught together one of us would have been called traitor even by our own countrymen. Daily, his leg seemed to be healing. Our tight wrappings seemed to have closed the gash together and my mother's ointment had worked its magic. Davoud called it a magic potion and asked how she made it - but I didn't know.'

'During the hot daytime we rigged up a sort of tent with the cloaks I had found, by spreading them across the tops of the boulders. But at night when it was so cold we wrapped them around ourselves. It was always hard to sleep. The ground was very hard and we were both so afraid of being discovered.'

'During the long days we talked and talked - about our families and homes - and how we lived in our own countries. He said his father was a very wealthy merchant and when there was peace sent ships to other lands far away and organised great caravans to Mecca carrying spices and silks. He knew the only way to make money was to live in peace with the Latins, just sell them what they wanted from our lands and take their money. But our different languages had always been a problem so when a sick, starving injured Norman French priest had been found lying in the road his father had taken him in. He was fed and nursed back to health. The priest who could both read and write had lived on with Davoud's family and was employed by his father to teach Davoud and his brother to speak, read and write our Norman- French language. Davoud's French was not too good but it was improving every day. It was better than my Arabic!'

'On the fifth morning, we decided that Davoud's leg was well enough to walk on though still very painful. But it was time to get back to our own people, me to the Knights Templar garrison in Jerusalem and Davoud to Damascus and his home. We still didn't know who had won that terrible battle at Hattin but Davoud said, looking over the battlefield at the hundreds of dead Franks, that he felt sure it had been Saladin's army.'

'We decided to set off at dusk. I filled our water skins from a spring we had found up on the hillside. We had no food left and were both very hungry. We decided that any food on the battlefield below was no longer good to eat.'

'He knew the land fairly well. He'd lived here all his life and had traveled with his uncle's cavalry and with his father's caravans. I didn't know the land at all and I had to get to Jerusalem. He took a stick and drew me a picture of the land. He marked the two hills where we were sheltering, with stones. These we had to climb up and over and down the other side to the lake in the valley. I remembered some of our foot soldiers trying to get to that lake the night before the battle when we had all been so thirsty. He then marked Damascus with a stone and Jerusalem with another. He was going North and I had to go South. He suggested I could go to Damascus with him but I said travelling together could be dangerous. Anyway, I wanted to get back to the barracks in Jerusalem and hoped to find my cousin and perhaps my friends.'

'We set off and struggled up the hill and started down the other side. The great lake at the bottom reflected the red sky of the setting sun as it slipped behind the hills. Davoud explained that that was the Sea of Galilea. As it began to get darker little lights appeared on the lake. "Fishermen." he said as we reached the lake side.'

'"You must keep the river on your left side all the way." said Davoud. "Walk along the bank. You will see Jerusalem ahead of you eventually but it will be a two day march."'

'The knights Templar had trained on the plains outside the walls of Jerusalem so I knew I would recognise it when I saw it but it was a sad parting from my friend.'

'"We will meet again sometime." he said and then grinned. "And thank you very much for my language lessons."'

'He handed me my sword back. It had been used to help him walk. His leg was very painful and he still could not straighten it forcing him to walk with a limp. I looked at my precious sword. He really needed it more than I did; in fact I don't think he could have walked without it. I handed it back, asking him to look after it.'

'"Perhaps I'll get it back one day!" I said.'

'Handing him a couple of cloaks, we hugged each other

Damascus, Hattin, Tiberias and
Jerusalem on a modern map.

and he set off. I watched him - a small limping figure walking away from me into the gathering darkness. I felt very lonely and hoped he would get home to Damascus. He should - he was an Arab in his own country - he stood a better chance than I did. I could only speak a little Arabic and I didn't really know the way and what's more it was now almost dark. I had water but was so hungry.'

'I set off. "Keep the river on your left!" he had said. "Walk along the bank." Let's hope I didn't fall into it in the dark!'

'I decided to walk until exhaustion forced me to stop which I did eventually, stopping when I caught my foot, tripped, and fell into a small hole. Picking myself up unhurt I decided that the small hole was a good place to sleep the night. So, wrapping myself in my cloaks, I curled up and fell asleep.'

'I woke at dawn very cold despite my two cloaks. I walked to the water's edge and sat down on the bank wondering how far I could go without food. However I had to get to Jerusalem so I set off. I walked for ages. The early morning sun was still low in the sky. Suddenly I smelt food. Someone was cooking FOOD! "What a fool!" I thought. My hunger was playing tricks with my mind and my nose, but walking on - yes - it was food and now I could also hear voices. As I got closer I dropped to my knees in the long grass. Men were talking around a fire in language I didn't understand. They could be

Latins. We spoke many languages. Perhaps men like me who had escaped from the battle. I crawled closer and lifted my head to see over the reeds.'

'Suddenly a hand grabbed the back of my cloak and hauled me to my feet. A big strong man holding a knife swung me round shouting to his companions at the fire. They all jumped up, knives drawn, looking around, perhaps thinking there were more of us. I must have fainted from fright and hunger for the next thing I knew I was lying on the grass next to the fire.'

'I sat up. One of the men gave me a drink of water and then a hunk of bread and fish. That was what I could smell earlier, cooking fish. Food had never tasted so good! One chap pointed at me and said "Frank?" I nodded. He said something to his friends and they all laughed. These men were not Latin Franks.'

'Then the men began arguing, angry, shouting. The man who had given me food seemed to be disagreeing with the others who were all shouting at once. I heard the word Damascus. In the end the man shrugged his shoulders and smiled at me in a sad sort of way and helped me to stand up. One of the others tied my hands and led me to the river bank where there were a couple of small fishing boats moored to the bank holding lots of fish in woven wooden baskets. I was pushed aboard one on them and we set off, the men rowing. Sadly for me we were going the wrong way! We were going North!'

'I said "Jerusalem?" One of them repeated "Jerusalem?" I nodded again. Laughing he yelled across to the others and said something I didn't understand, "Al-Quds!" Again they all laughed.'

CHAPTER 13

YOUNG MAN FOR SALE

'The morning wore on as the men rowed up river in silence. The sun still low in the sky, there was a cool wind blowing. They had taken my two precious cloaks and my leather jerkin off me, probably intending to sell them but when the man with the friendly face realised I was shivering he wrapped one cloak round my shoulders. His friend rebuked him with sharp angry words for his kindness but I was allowed to keep the cloak.'

'We finally landed the two boats at a little clearing. People, mostly women, were waiting, standing in groups, and the men having clambered ashore, began to sell fish from their round baskets. I sat on the ground watching. Eventually, returning to the boats, we set off again.'

'The sun was high in the sky when we reached a big town. I was roughly dragged off the boat with my hands still tied in front of me and marched through the city gates onto the busy streets. We walked for a while through the noisy market and then on down a long road away from the town. At the bottom, blocking our way was a wall higher than two men and topped with curved metal spikes. One of my captors banged on a big wood and metal door set in the wall. A small square panel was opened and a face looked out from behind a metal grill. He listened to my captors then looked at me. The grill was closed and we waited. Finally the huge door opened and as we walked through we were immediately surrounded by six guards dressed in grey tunics, trousers and wide yellow sashes around their waists. They each carried a large curved scimitar.

'The door crashed to behind us. I was terrified! So I suspect were the fishermen and yet, looking around, we were in a beautiful garden filled with beds of flowers, the colours of which I had never seen before. Fountains played into sparkling pools full of golden fish. Somebody very rich lived here. No wonder he had metal spikes on his walls. I stopped and stared around me but was roughly pushed towards a house and what a house! It seemed to be made out of pink shining stone. Two great pillars were holding up a carved roof over a porch which sheltered a big heavy wooden door.'

'The door was suddenly opened by two men who bowed to a third man as he walked between them onto the wide steps. He wore a red turban and a long yellow coat that hung down to the ground on either side of his great fat belly. His white tunic and trousers were of beautiful embroidered shiny material. He was a small man - smaller than me - but he was so fat that he looked like a pig's bladder on legs. His face was so fat that his eyes, almost lost, peeped out of tiny slits above his round fat cheeks. He had no neck - just rolls of fat hanging under his chin. He looked like a slug. I hated the look of him.'

'The fishermen, having pushed me forward onto my knees, bowed to him and one of them began to speak. The little fat man waddled down two of the three steps and stood in front of me. He waved his hand indicating I should stand. He grabbed one of my arms - I think to decide how thin I was. His fat podgy fingers were covered in rings. I then had to open my mouth and he looked at my teeth. I felt like a horse up for sale, for this is what my father would do when buying a horse. He spoke to my captors who bowed again and he turned and walked back into the house. We waited. Two men finally came out. They were both dressed in the grey uniform and they each carried a large scimitar fastened to their belts. One handed a pouch of money to the fishermen whilst the other put a rope around my neck and dragged me away. I realised I had been sold.'

'The guard took me to a small stone hut and pushed me inside. It was not much bigger than my dog's kennel. I was forced to sit with my back to the wall with my knees bent up under my chin. The rope around my neck was fastened to a ring in the wall above my head. It was so tight I felt I would choke. I couldn't move. The door was banged shut and I was in complete darkness.'

'I spent a miserable night unable to stretch my legs with my head tied to the wall. What was worse I was desperately thirsty. Each time I fell asleep my head would fall forward tightening the rope around my throat.'

'Morning came at last. I could see daylight through cracks in the tiny wooden prison door. Eventually my box was opened and somebody pushed in a hunk of flat bread and a cup of water. Later the guards came and dragged me out. I couldn't stand up or straighten my legs for ages. I lay curled up on the ground and one of the men kicked me.'

'Later I was taken out of the garden into the town being led by the rope round my neck which was tied to the saddle of one of the mounted guards. Reaching the town square I saw on the ground, huddled together, what looked like piles of rags. Another guard, who had been sitting nearby, went among these rags, kicking at them and lashing them with his whip. They were not rags. They were men curled up like animals, fast asleep.

'As they pulled themselves together and struggled to their feet I realised that they were all chained together by their necks. Each man wore a metal collar. A chain was threaded through a loop and passed on to the man behind through the loop on his collar and so on joining the whole column of prisoners together. I was added to the end of the line and tied on to the collar of the fellow in front of me by my neck rope. These men had been walking for days. Someone came along with a container of water and a cup and gave each man a drink. The lead man's chain was then tied to the lead horse's saddle and we all set off to where I did not know but we walked for two days. It was two days of hell on earth.'

'At night we camped. The guards had a fire but we just huddled together for warmth. We were given only dry bread and water to eat and drink. I called out once "Does anyone speak my language?" but one of the guards came and clouted me on the head. After a while a voice whispered "Aye, lad! But we're not allowed to talk. There are two Franks here - three now, with you." The voice belonged to a man two ahead of me on the chain. I asked him where we were going. "To Damascus, we think to be sold at the market there. Big slave market in Damascus."'

'"But they can't sell us." I said. "We don't belong to them."'

'"We do now, boy!"'

'We reached Damascus at the end of the next day. We were so tired. The only time we had stopped was to give the guards and horses a rest. Most of the others had no shoes and their feet were torn and bleeding. My boots had gone to a fisherman but he had exchanged them for his old pair of sandals. I was lucky.'

'Damascus was a big wealthy town, well dressed people walked on wide pavements fringed by high walls probably hiding beautiful houses and gardens like the one I had seen a few days before. We, this line of dirty men chained together, were forced to walk in a wide middle track used by horses, camels, donkeys and fine horse-drawn chariots. We reached a market filled with stalls, merchants selling fruit, meat, bread and some carrying baskets of hot food. One stall we passed was draped with brightly coloured shiny cloth. How my mother would have loved a length for a gown and how we would have loved some of the food being sold.'

'Our guards drove us on with little chance to see around us. We had to keep up with the man in front as, being joined to each other's neck halter, we were at risk of being choked. Finally, at dusk, we halted once again outside a big wood and metal door set in a huge wall. The lead guard banged on the door which was opened and we all trudged into a large round compound protected by high walls again topped with metal spikes. At one end was a huge trough of water which was fed by a spring. We all dashed to the trough, all so thirsty. Then we sat in a group on the dusty ground.'

'One of the guards cut the rope which was around my neck and led me away to what looked like a blacksmith's shop. The smith measured my neck with his hands and chose a wide metal collar from a selection hanging on his wall. He fitted it and fastened it at the back with a bolt. It was cold and heavy, resting on my shoulders, but not as tight as the rope had been. He then bolted a similar piece of metal around each ankle and each wrist and threaded a length of chain through a loop on the neck halter down through loops on both wrists and finally to loops at my ankles. He then measured the chain between my feet and joined the ends together with much hammering.'

'The guard who had been chattering to the Smith all this time now indicated that I should follow him. Had my plight not been so tragic it might have been laughable. Because my elbows were not quite straight, the weight of my arms was hanging on my neck pulling me forward. The short length of chain joining my ankles forced me to take little hobbling steps thus causing me to almost fall on my face. I was taken to a long tunnel-like prison room. On benches down each side sat men who were chained. There must have been two score (40) of us. Nobody spoke but all looked up at me as I entered. I sat down on the bench and was fastened to the wall by yet another chain hooked onto my neck iron. And there I sat. The only daylight, coming in through the metal grill doorway at one end of the tunnel, was fading.'

'A voice whispered in my ear. "I think we've missed supper!"'

'Turning my head with difficulty, I realised it was the Frank I had met on the march. He said his name was Jake and had been taken prisoner after the great battle. "Cheer up, Lad, we're alive!" he smiled, but I couldn't stop the tears rolling down my face. I hoped he couldn't see them.'

'That was to be the first of six nights in that terrible place. I chipped a mark with my wrist iron on the wall behind me each sunset. We could lean against the wall but proper sleep was impossible. We just cat napped. There was a constant chinking of chains as men tried to get some comfort. Some would cry out in their sleep - perhaps I did.'

'We were taken out twice a day. At dawn we were given bread and water and at sunset we were given a kind of porridge and allowed water from the trough. "They have to feed us." Jake explained. "We're worth nothing dead and buyers like healthy slaves. At least they like them standing up."'

'Walking was difficult. Eventually I learned to bow my head and lean forward. This allowed me more chain at my feet for walking. Trouble was the heavy collar felt as though it would break my neck. Also, the solid rough metal leg irons rubbed holes in my ankles, making them bleed. It was a sad miserable time. Nobody knew what was to become of us.'

'On the seventh morning there was more noise than usual, men shouting, laughing, the sounds of horses. The grill was flung open and we were marched out into the compound as usual and fed and watered. The guards then lined us up against the wall one behind the other (I was pushed to the end of the line) and they proceeded to chain us together by our neck irons. We noticed that the guards were all dressed alike in a uniform of light blue tunic and dark blue breeches. They had a wide sash around their waists that shone like gold and a matching turban headdress. We watched as four of them mounted their horses whilst the rest of them lined up on each side of our column. The gates were opened and we shuffled out walking towards the town of Damascus.'

'It was busy, so many people, women with baskets

going to market, men with donkeys and camels loaded with goods. It must have been market day. Some stopped and stood aside to let us pass. We were again made to walk in the road reserved for the animals whilst our guards walked on the cleaner path. So much noise of people shouting. It was still early morning the sun not yet really up. A group of horses passed us. Because of my chains I was unable to lift my head to look up at the riders but could see from my level that they were beautiful horses. Their coats shone and their tails were long and well brushed.'

'All I could see of the riders were their beautiful leather riding boots and the edges of their long cloaks hanging down over the horse's flanks. 'Must be very rich!' I muttered to myself as we shambled along and I thought about home and my father's beautiful horses. I also wondered where my cousin was. Jake had said the Lord Saladin had won the battle and had conquered Jerusalem sometime over the next days. Perhaps cousin William had escaped.'

'Ahead of us there were buildings and walking towards them were lines of men chained together like us. This must be the market.'

'By now I could hardly walk. The leg irons had cut their way into the tops of my feet and had taken all the skin off my ankles. I looked down at the feet of the men ahead of me. Theirs were just the same.'

'Once again we reached a high wall and we were herded into a huge compound through great iron gates. Then we were ordered to sit which we gladly did - a difficult manouevre - sitting down when joined to the next chap by the neck, running the risk of choking ourselves together with the men in front and behind.'

'There seemed to be hundreds of men like ourselves joined by rope or chain at the neck standing or sitting in groups, their watchful guards close by. Our guards were chatting to the fellows guarding the next group. These men were dressed in red and yellow silk. This sale must have been a very rich affair as guards all over the compound seemed to be wearing their best uniforms. It was like a feast day at home - everyone in their best clothes.'

'From the very large building within the compound came the noise and babble of men's voices. Such a noise, laughing, talking, then suddenly there was the crash of a gong and slowly the noise stopped and all was quiet. "The sale is starting!" whispered Jake. A man's voice could be heard and then clapping and shouting from a room full of people. Then all quiet again. We watched as the first line of men was assembled below a flight of steps up into the building. The men were separated and were led one at a time up the steps. We could hear the man's voice shouting and answering shouts from the crowd. Sometimes a voice would shout something and everybody would laugh. Then the gong sounded. Men clapped and cheered and another prisoner was led up the steps. Those sold must have been going out at another door.'

'Our lot was the third batch to be pushed forward. They seemed to be selling men at a fast rate. At each strike of the gong another man was pushed up the steps. We stood at the bottom waiting our turn. Our guards removed the chain that joined our neck irons. I was last in the line and terrified. Jake turned and said "God be with you, perhaps we'll meet again sometime." As his turn came he turned again and grinned, then walked up the steps and disappeared into the building. I could hear men shouting, one at a time, each I suppose bidding a higher price. I had once been to a horse sale with my father but I never thought they could sell people like this.'

'The gong sounded and a cheer went up. It was now my turn. I was so scared I felt sick and tripped up the steps. A guard pulled me to my feet and pushed me through the doorway. What a sight met my eyes. I was standing on a raised platform like a stage. Below me lay a huge room filled with men all looking up at me. Those at the front sat in gilded chairs with soft red seats. Those behind I think, sat on long benches but there were many buyers standing at the back jostling each other to see the stage. The room was very hot.'

'At one side of this stage sat a man at a table, writing. At the other stood the biggest man I had ever seen. He was standing beside a big metal gong and holding what seemed to be a padded hammer. He was black and naked to the waist but wore a pair of magnificent long yellow trews and a wide silver sash round his waist, obviously a slave as he too wore a metal neck iron. Another man in fine silk garments was taking a drink from a goblet at the table. He said something to his audience and they laughed as he walked across the stage to me and prodded me with a horsewhip. He stared at me and said "Frank?" I nodded. He then said in my own language "How - many - years - are - you?'" I was so surprised I had to think. "Seventeen." I said. He thought for a moment and then turning spoke to the audience probably telling them what a good buy I was. He tore the sleeve from what was left of my ragged dirty tunic perhaps to show them what strong arms I had. I didn't feel very strong.'

'The men started bidding first one then another. The auctioneer danced about the stage shouting and encouraging more bids. The audience laughed at his antics. Somebody shouted a bid and everybody cheered. Then all went quiet. I looked down at the hundreds of faces below. This was not happening to me. My feet were chained together. My wrists were chained together. The whole thing was a nightmare. I would surely wake up at any minute.'

'The auctioneer was still prancing about trying to get more bids. He pointed to the man who had made the last offer and raised his hand. He gazed slowly all round the room. The black slave too had raised his arm. There was complete silence. I closed my eyes waiting for the crash of the gong. Then out of the silence a voice at the back of the hall shouted. The hall erupted into cheering and clapping and men turned in their seats to see who had spoken. He had obviously outbid the last fellow by some considerable margin. The auctioneer clapped and bowed to the bidder. I was now able to pick him out as the people around him were laughing, joking and slapping him on the back. He too was laughing and gave a little mock bow. The gong sounded.'

'I was sold!'

CHAPTER 14

SOLD!

'A guard seized me by my neck iron and pushed me towards the side of the stage and down the steps. I stumbled out into the hall down the side of the seated men. The next man for sale was already on the stage behind me. I was forgotten. The metal around my ankles was biting into the open wounds they had caused and the pain was intense. I tried not to cry but I know the tears were streaming down my face. I was so angry. How dare these people sell me? I was the son of a Duke.

'The men, crowded in the room, were already cheering and jeering, orchestrated once again by the auctioneer trying to sell his next victim. Still unable to lift my head when walking, I shuffled, neck bent, to the back of the room steered by the guard. I was halted at a pair of beautiful leather riding boots. I lifted my arms and my head to look up at the face of the man who had bought me. He was a tall slim man, taller than me with wide powerful shoulders. He had a lean handsome face with dark smiling eyes. His grey beard was trimmed to a neat point below his chin and his wide moustache turned up at the sides giving his face a permanent grin.'

'He handed the guard some coins and turning, guided me out into the brilliant sunshine. I remember I was puzzled. He didn't push or pull me. He just held my elbow guiding, walking slowly beside me out into the sunshine. One walked very slowly in shackles and chains. The yard was hot now under the blazing sun and lots of men like me, already sold, were being dragged away stumbling, leg irons still in place. Some tied to a master's saddle by his neck or wrist irons. One poor fellow was being tied face down across the back of a camel like a sack of corn. I hoped it wasn't Jake.'

'We walked across the compound into a blacksmith's shop and there the man spoke to the Smith who had almost fallen over himself to bow to my new master. He seemed surprised at what he had been told to do but, bowing again, he set to work. First he cut the chain joining my wrists to my neck. It fell to the floor with a clatter. I was suddenly able to stand up straight; oh - the relief! Then he cut the chain joining my feet and removed the shackles from my ankles. Next he removed the irons from my wrists and finally the cruel neck collar. I nodded to the smith with tears streaming down my face. He smiled at me. I tried to remember the words for thank you in arabic but couldn't.'

'The Smith was paid and I followed my master out into the yard once again and over towards a group of four beautifully groomed and saddled horses waiting patiently beside a couple of men dressed in rich garments. They turned as we approached. One of them laughed and walked towards me. He had a shocking limp. I looked into his face. This man so beautifully dressed I hardly recognised him. DAVOUD!!!!!!!!!!!!! We threw our arms around each other both sobbing. "We passed you this morning as they took you to market." he said. "I recognised you at the end of the column from your black clothes and the back of your head. You still have a mass of dried blood on the back of your hair from your wound."'

'His father, for it was he who had bought me, separated

us, laughing. A crowd had gathered around, I suppose amazed to see a well-known rich man's son embracing the dirty tattered slave. I was helped onto one of the horses, again to the amazement of the guards and crowd, and we rode away out of the compound. '

'Davoud's home was a palace surrounded by high stone walls. The gardens were ablaze with beautiful flowers, shady trees and sparkling fountains and pools of water filled with coloured fish. I wondered if heaven was like this, so different to the prison where I had spent those awful days. Apart from the birds and the fountains there was no sound.'

'As soon as we arrived I was taken away by a man servant, my old filthy uniform removed and I was put into a bath of warm scented water. My hair was cut and washed and my beard shaved. The warm water soothed the pain in my throbbing ankles and feet. I was given a robe and taken to a room overlooking the garden. It was cool and there was a breeze from the garden disturbing the soft white drapes at the open doors. The floor was of polished stone, which I later learned was called marble. It reflected everything like a pool of still water. I lay down on a bed covered with soft sheets. The man servant came in and gave me a warm drink of something that tasted like honey. I don't remember falling asleep but Davoud said afterwards that I had slept for almost two days.'

'Over the next few weeks life really was like living in paradise. His mother was very beautiful. She had long black hair which she usually wore in a long plait covered by a soft scarf. She often wore a cover over her face too, showing only her eyes. I thought it was a pity to hide such a lovely face but Davoud said it was their custom.'

'Davoud and I swapped stories of our adventures after we had parted that awful day. He, being the son of a well known rich merchant, had managed to co-opt help from the master of a caravan traveling to Damascus, and had reached home in safety.'

'My story was much more exciting and the family gathered to hear it translated for them by Davoud. His father, laughing, said we were a couple of hot headed young pups who should both have stayed at home. We both agreed but then his father banged his fist on the table and seemed to get very angry. Davoud said he had said that war was wrong. Men should live in peace. Too many young men had died leaving only old men, women and children. Lives lost - wasted. We, Davoud and I, remembering that terrible sight of the battlefield and of the hundreds of dead men and animals, both agreed.'

'We also agreed when his father said that we were lucky to be alive, however I pointed out to him that I had him to thank for my being alive, as he must have paid a lot of money for me at the auction market. He came over to me and put his arm around my shoulders and said he would have paid twice my weight in gold if he had needed to. I had saved his son's life. I said that that was probably more to do with my mother's magic ointment, at which everybody laughed. "Yes, but you were there, my son!" he said. "You dragged him off the battlefield despite the fact that he was your enemy. You found shelter, food and water and tended his wound. Talking about magic ointment, I would love to know how your mother made it." I said I really had no idea although I remembered honey and salt were part of the mixture together with special plants.'

131

'As the weeks passed I slowly recovered. The wounds around my ankles made by the leg irons healed although I still carry the scars to this day.'

'I met the priest, Pierre, who had taught Davoud and his younger brother to speak my language. He was a young man who had come to Outremer on a pilgrimage with a group of priests. They had been attacked and robbed by a band of outlaws. Some of their party had been killed. He, Pierre, having been left for dead outside the walls of Damascus, had been found by a servant of Davoud's father. He had carried him back to the house where he had been nursed back to health and had lived and worked ever since.'

'One day I asked Davoud's father if he knew what had happened after the battle of Hattin. He said that the Mighty Saladin and his army had won the day. Anyone of the Frankish army who was left standing had been sold into slavery. Many of the knights had been ransomed but as always, any Knight Templar who had survived the battle had been executed next day. I wondered what had happened to my cousin William.'

'I loved the life there at Davoud's beautiful house; I loved the warm sunshine and blue skies. I had the use of a lovely black stallion called Abar and Davoud and I spent many happy hours riding outside the city walls. Yet, despite all this, I wanted to go home. My parents didn't know if I was alive or dead and I longed to see them again. I missed silly little things - my home with its smoky wood fires - the lovely warm smell of our horses in the stables on a cold day - the magic of a frosty morning - galloping across our hillside - the whole countryside white with frost - the grass crunching beneath my horse's hooves - my dog, Bran, dashing along beside me. I could never repay these lovely people for saving me from slavery and nursing me back to health. I owed them so much yet despite all this I began to realise that I had to go home.'

'Davoud begged me to stay; he had a beautiful cousin he said who would make me a beautiful wife and I could work for his father and become very rich. I promised I would come back one day.'

'Plans for my departure were made. At the end of the month Davoud's father was sending a shipload of silks and spices to Malta and Genoa. He said he would send Pierre and me on this ship and drop us off at Genoa. He asked me if there was anything I would like to take home. I suddenly remembered the stall selling that shiny cloth the day we trudged to the slave market. So I asked for a length of the blue cloth, which I now know is called silk, for my mother and one of the fabulous Arabic leather sword belts for my father. He smiled "And nothing for you?" he asked. I explained that I thought I had taken enough from them already.'

'It was a sad day as we said our goodbyes. Davoud handed me a pair of magnificent leather boots and parcels containing the silk for my mother which had been chosen by Davoud's mother and the sword belt for my father. I was lost for words - I had nothing to give them. He then handed both Pierre and me a heavy woolen cloak lined with sheep's wool. "These will keep you warm at night on the boat and when you reach your own cold land." he said and added "Please come back one day." I promised I would.'

'I put on my new boots and put my parcels into a sack

on my back. Davoud's father was standing waiting to say his goodbyes. "I feel I am loosing a son. We shall miss you, Guy, and this" he said taking a leather case from a table beside him and placing it into my hands "is my thanks for giving me my son."'

'I gazed at his gift - a magnificent shiny leather case tooled and dyed in red and blue patterns like feathers. It was about the length of my forearms and slightly wider at the top with a strap attached enabling it to be carried over the shoulder and across the chest. I slipped the strap over my head and the case sat comfortably at my waist over my hip. "I have never seen such a beautiful leather case." I said "Thank you so much." I was already planning to carry my other gifts in it when Davoud said "Well open it." He looked at his father and laughed. "Open it?" I repeated. "Yes! The gift is inside!" he said.'

'I lifted it off my shoulder and released two metal clips which held a flap at the top in place. The sight that met my eyes as I opened the case I shall never forget. It was the glint of a solid gold handle nestling in a bed of red silk. It looked like the handle of a sword but in GOLD? I carefully pulled it out of the leather case and sat on the floor with it across my knees. It wasn't a sword but a solid gold miniature scimitar complete with a silver and gold scabbard encrusted with pearls, rubies and emeralds. These jewels were in swirling patterns and set in frames of pearls. I could never have imagined anything so fabulous or so beautiful.'

'I looked up at Davoud and his father. I was in shock. They both laughed. "I don't know what to say." I stammered. "A true scimitar" began his father, "is a powerful weapon." He didn't need to tell me this. I'd seen them at work. "This one however," he continued, "can never be used in anger and I hope it will serve as a reminder that people can live in peace. Trade brings peace and makes us rich. Wars make us poor and kill off our young men. Oh! And by the way, here's another thing you must have." He handed me my grandfather's sword. "Let us hope that it too can live in peace."'

'Davoud, his father and a couple of servants rode with us to the gates of Damascus where Pierre and I joined a caravan of merchants making for the coastal port of Haifa. There, his father's beautiful ship waited for us. Other merchants were using the ship and we were treated like royalty.'

'We finally landed at Genoa after many days at sea and having been put ashore set off to travel home to France. We bought horses for the journey. It was a long way but we were in no great hurry. I had been given gold coins by Davoud's father for our journey so we were able to pay for food and lodging on the way. We eventually reached my uncle's home near Rouen where I had spent my youth. My uncle and his family were delighted to see me and hear of my adventures. His younger son, my Knight Templar cousin, had never returned so I expect he died at the battle of Hattin.'

'I was now longing to get home and so within a week, my uncle got us and our horses onto a boat across the Channel. From Dover we traveled to London and then home to my house near Wallingford. I stopped on the road below the house and we walked up hill to my home, hoping to surprise everyone. My dog saw me first. He was lying on the path on sentry duty overlooking the hillside in front of the house but the sound of our boots on the grass alerted him. He growled, ears flat on his head. I called his name. 'BRAN! Come!' I had a special whistle to call him. He did a double take and then with a yelp of shear delight he rushed down the hill. What a glorious welcome.'

'Many more welcomes followed. My parents had thought me dead. There was much feasting as friends came to see me and hear my story. Mother had a beautiful gown made from the blue silk and my father found all sorts of reasons to wear his sword belt with or without his sword! One favourite was that his breeches were too big! They decided they would try and contact Davoud's family and thank them for what they had done for me. My beautiful scimitar now has pride of place in my room together with my grandfather's sword. My father has promised to build a little chapel at the edge of the wood where they will eventually rest on the altar together - both at peace.'

'It is now almost a year since we got back. Pierre, who incidentally is now the family priest, my father's scribe and secretary, was persuaded by my mother to write down my story as it had happened before I forgot it - as though I ever could. It has taken us six winter months - me talking - Pierre slowly writing it down and here it is, finished. I hope somebody will read it one day.'

'When the crusading and the fighting in Outremer is over and people are living in peace, when it is safe to go and visit again, Pierre and I intend to go back to Damascus on our own pilgrimage.'

Christopher closed his manuscript. Taking out a large handkerchief he blew his nose very loudly. Guy and I sat very still both lost in our own thoughts.

136

'Well, we did,' he said.

'Did what?' asked Chris looking at Guy.

'We read his story!'

'Yes we did, but think about it. Up to a couple of years ago when the box fell out of the chimney, nobody had seen this story let alone read it since the 1600s when somebody rewrote it.' said Chris lifting the lid of the box. He took out a manuscript. 'This is a list of the treasure as it was then and also, in this tiny pouch, is a key. I wonder what lock this fits - probably never know.' he said replacing them.

'It would make a good story.' I said walking over to the fireplace to get another look at the scimitar and sword carved into the wooden plaque over the mantelpiece.

'Well, come on you two! Your mother will have your supper ready.'

We walked back to the house. I looked down across the hill my head still full of Guy's story.

'This is where he used to gallop down the valley on his horse with his dog.'

'Yes,' said Guy 'and I've seen this hillside and those trees covered with frost on a winter's day and felt the grass crunch as I walked on it. It's funny! He talked about this hillside and this is it. We're standing on it.'

'Pity they lost the treasure.' I said. 'Wouldn't it be great to be able to see or touch that scimitar?' We went in for supper.

CHAPTER 15

A SECRET ROOM

I think it was Wednesday and as I got dressed, the rain was slashing against my bedroom window. I realised that I still hadn't asked Liz to stitch the buckle on my sandal; it was now very loose. We sat at breakfast wondering what to do with our day.

'It would rain.' I said.

'I know!' said Guy suddenly. 'I've got a great idea! Let's go down the passages, is that OK Mum?'

'Yes of course. Just remember to prop open the door.'

'We will!'

'See if you can find the secret room.' she laughed.

'Hey! Yeh! That would be a good trick. Dad and Aunt Sue never did. In fact, nobody has ever found it.' Guy said.

After breakfast we trudged up the wide shiny wooden staircase to the library. It was a wonderful thrill as we stood in front of that old dark wooden paneling. I watched Guy place the flat of his hand on the square panel and saw it move sideways as he turned his hand. He grinned over his shoulder as we heard that little click and the whirring noise, a bit like the sound of a bicycle chain when it's pedalled backwards. The secret door swung open and we propped it in place with Henry.

I have thought very carefully about what happened next and although I must tell it very slowly, blow by painful blow, in fact, it all happened in a matter of seconds. Guy handed me a torch. Turning his on he set off at a fast run shouting over his shoulder 'Race you to the cellar!' I, taken completely by surprise, shouted 'I thought we were going to look for ....' But by this time he was out of earshot, almost at the end of the passage.

I tried to turn on my torch and started to run but the torch didn't light up. I stopped - shook it - banged it on my other hand - still no light. Guy by now had gone down the first flight of steps at the end and the passage was in darkness. I stepped back into the library still trying to get my silly torch to light. Suddenly it did - great - I started to sprint at speed down the passage. Then - disaster - I felt my sandal strap come loose. The buckle had come off. As my foot went up behind me my sandal slipped partially off, by now remember, I was running fast. As I plunged my foot to the floor taking my next step I stamped with all my weight onto the hard back of my sandal. A hot stab of pain shot up through my foot and up the back of my leg.

My brain was saying, 'Do not do that again!' but my legs were still running. In trying to lift my foot and hop - and trying to stop - and trying not to stand on that foot again - I lost my balance and hit the wall with a crash. I dropped the torch. It went out. Still going forward, I hit my head and my shoulder with some considerable force on the panelling. I saw stars! The pain in my shoulder was awful. Having crashed with all my weight, I slid down the wall to the floor in total darkness, leaning with all my weight on the panelling. Then, suddenly, the wall behind me seemed to melt and I was rolling over backwards, falling.

The only thing I could remember afterwards was a click. When I stopped falling I was on a hard floor curled up holding my head, terrified. When nothing else happened I carefully sat up. All was quiet but I was in total darkness. My head was throbbing, my shoulder hurt and I was sure I would never walk again, my heel hurt so much. Sitting on the floor I stretched my arms out in front and to the sides but I couldn't find a wall or my torch. However, I wasn't getting up to look because it was too dark and things might start moving again. Guy would be back with his torch any minute but I did wonder where the wall had gone. I had a headache and felt a bit sick.

I sat in the darkness it seemed for ages and then - magic - I heard Guy calling my name. His voice got closer and then fainter again. Where was he? He must be down on the lower passage. Hope he still had his torch; he'd fall over me otherwise. I heard him again getting closer shouting my name. 'I'M HERE!' I shouted.

'WHERE?'

'HERE, ON THE TOP PASSAGE!'

'NO! YOU'RE NOT - DON'T BE ROTTEN - WHERE ARE YOU?'

'I'm here!' I shouted, 'I fell over. Bring a torch - I can't see.'

'Oh Luke - you're NOT in the passage!'

'Then where am I?' I was suddenly very scared.

'I've found your torch. Listen. Shout at me again.'

'GUY!' I shouted with all my strength.

'Luke! Are you listening? I think you're on the other side of this wall.' He began banging on the panelling. 'Can you hear that?'

I stood up. 'Yes!' I answered, 'Keep banging.' I started to stumble towards the noise - arms outstretched in front of me. It only took about three careful steps - I was fully expecting to fall down a dark hole or something - when I found the wall I'd lost. It felt cold like stone. I banged on it.

'Oh thank goodness!' shouted Guy. 'You are on the other side of the wall. 'How did you get in there? Where's the door? Oh Boy, LISTEN! STAY THERE - I'M GOING TO GET MUM.'

I wondered where he thought I could possibly go! Anyway, carefully holding on to the wall, I turned and sat down with my back to it. I felt safer with something to lean on. The floor felt like stone. It was cold. Absolute black dark and absolute silence. And then,at last, sounds thank goodness. Guy was back.

'Luke!' It was Liz. 'Luke! Are you alright?'

'Yes!' I shouted. I would tell them about my injuries when they got me out.

'I've sent Guy to get Chris. I'm trying all these panels. One of them must work the mechanics of a door. Can you see anything in there?'

'No. It's pitch black.'

'We'll have you out in no time.'

'Good!' I shouted although I rather doubted that. I could hear her knocking on the panelling and then 'Luke! Can you hear me?'

'Yes!'

'Guy's back with Chris and a couple of hurricane lamps.'

'Hello Luke!' It was Chris. 'What happened?'

'I don't really know. I tripped and hit the wall and then a door must have opened. I fell through somewhere and sort of fell over backwards.'

'OK. Where are you now?'

'Sitting on the floor - leaning on a wall.'

'Is there any wooden panelling on the wall?'

'No. It's hard cold stone.'

'That's good. Right - now! Stand up and face the wall. Walk to your right three or four steps touching the wall. Any wooden panels?'

'No.' I answered.

'Good - now go back to where you started and walk to your left still holding on to the wall.'

I did as he said and suddenly felt the wooden panels under my hands and taking another step sideways I hit a wall. 'I've found the panels' I shouted 'and I've come to the corner of the room.'

'That's great - wonderful - good lad! Now. How many panels can you feel side by side?'

I ran my hands over the wood. 'Three!' I shouted.

'OK. That must be the door.'

I heard muffled sounds and voices. I waited and then the click and the whirring of a chain! A chink of brilliant light appeared down the wall. The door was open. I stood back and heard Chris say 'Careful. The mechanism and chains could all be rusted and could all collapse.' The panel, which was the door, was pushed open very carefully and the relief was wonderful. There they all stood staring in at me. Guy was first into the room and promptly fell sprawling with a yell at my feet. With the help of the lamps Chris realised that there was a step down into the room from the passage, which Guy had missed! This was why I had had that awful feeling of falling after I had hit the wall.

Chris and Liz stepped carefully down into the room bringing the hurricane lamps with them. What a sight we saw! It had a stone floor and partly whitewashed walls although much of the walls were covered with book-laden shelves. There was a table against another wall and two chairs. One of the chairs was askew at the table as though some person had just moved it aside to stand up. I pointed this out to Chris.

'Yes' he said 'but not just - about 300 years ago!'

'But what about the little boy that got locked in here?'

'Not in here.' said Chris 'According to the records he got into a room on the lower passage probably directly under this one. Might be able to find that one now, thanks to you, Luke.'

On the desk was an inkwell with what looked like a feather sitting in it although the ink had long dried out. There were other feathers lying untidily on the desk.

'Those are quill pens made from goose feathers.' said Chris. There was also a box with a sloping lid, but it was locked.

'Don't move or touch anything.' said Chris looking at a mass of scrolls in little pigeonholes which were attached to the wall over the desk. 'I want Tim and Andrew to see this and we'll get some photographs done of the room just as we found it. They will want to record and catalogue everything just as it is. Also I feel those quill pens will probably disintegrate to dust when they are touched. We'll have to get these scrolls to the museum for treatment before we can unroll them or they will probably fall to bits too. Wish we could open that box though' he said. 'Pity - no key!' And then his face lit up. 'Wait a minute! Wait a minute! That KEY.'

'The little key you found in the chimney box!' said Guy.

'YES! Oh if only - could we be so lucky? Don't anybody move - I'll go and get it.'

We did move. We wandered round the room looking at the books that lined the back wall. There was a framed portrait on one wall of a lady and two children.

'I wonder who they were?' said Liz. 'This furniture was probably made at the time of Queen Elizabeth 1. Tim and Andrew will be over the moon when they see all this. I did say "See if you could find the secret room!" I never expected you to. Can you imagine your Dad's face when he sees this!' She grinned at Guy.

'Well, Luke found it!' replied Guy.

She put her arm round my shoulder. 'Yes, poor chap,' she said 'We've all been so excited about what we have found that we forgot what an awful fright you must have had.'

'I was a bit scared!' I admitted. 'It was so dark.' "Bit scared" was a bit of a porky really. I had been terrified.

'And where is your sandal?' she asked seeing my bare foot.

'I don't know - in the passage somewhere I guess.

The buckle came off as I was running. That's what tripped me up.'

Chris came running back. 'Got it!' he said. 'I also phoned Andrew and Tim. They are on their way. I've brought an oilcan to oil the door mechanism. Don't want it cracking up on us. Now!' he said with great glee 'Let's see if we can open the box!'

The key did fit and we all sighed with relief. We all crowded round.

'Well! No treasure!' said Chris as he lifted the lid but lying flat in the box was a poem written on a small piece of what looked like yellow brown cloth.

'Is that paper?' Liz asked.

'I think so.' said Chris. 'Yes, but I don't want to touch it.'

'What does it say?' Guy asked. Chris held the lamp higher and started to read.

'At octo on octo of octo
When rainbows merrily prance
At the baptism of blood and fire
Or when swallows cease their dance
And tall shadows gloom the mire
Here weapons in lasting peace will lie
But mark well my words You Sirs
Lest I should die.'

'Oh dear! And whatever does that mean and who wrote it, I wonder?' said Liz.

'I don't know!' said Chris. 'Go and get me a piece of paper and a pencil from the library please, Guy. I'll copy it and try to work it out. One thing is for sure! It was written a long time ago, he's talking about peaceful weapons. This can only mean the sword and the scimitar; they've always been known as 'Peaceful Weapons' even on the family crest. I think somebody is telling us where they are but I don't know - I just can't answer it. I wonder if it was written by Harry before he escaped to France?' He carefully copied the poem down and closed the box. 'Bit of a conundrum - that!'

Tim and Andrew arrived together and, with their mouths wide open, their faces were a picture. Both came armed with cameras and flashlights.

'I hope nobody has touched anything.' said Tim looking at Guy and me.

'Not a thing, Uncle Tim!'

'We might even get dates from the dust. Gosh when was this room last closed?'

'I've touched something ! I've opened this box." said Chris lifting the lid for them both to see the poem.

'Oh - er!' muttered Andrew. 'I'd like the answer to that little puzzle!'

'I'll give you a copy.' said Chris. 'You can have a go at solving it. In fact we can all try solving it!'

'Just think! This room has been quietly sleeping here as we see it now for possibly three hundred years.' said Timothy sitting down on the step of the doorway waiting for Andrew to set up a mass of lighting for the photos.

'Come on boys!' said Liz. 'Let's go and leave these men and get some lunch. You can have another look tomorrow.' It was then that Liz noticed I was limping as we walked down the corridor. My heel was very bruised and painful and I was forced to walk on my toes. I had a lump on my forehead where it and the wall had collided and I had a very painful shoulder. 'I'm so sorry you're so wounded but if you hadn't hit that wall doing forty miles an hour, we would never have found that secret room.'

'Look! Here is your sandal.' she added. My heel was very painful; in fact I limped for days afterwards.

. . . .

The men folk agreed to get together on Thursday afternoon and pool all their information. Liz was having everyone to supper that evening. Guy had a bright idea. 'If it's fine, why don't we get Granddad's tent and we'll camp out that night! We can cook our own supper on the gas burner and leave all the grown-ups to their party.'

There was a lot of activity on Thursday morning. Tim took all the scrolls to the museum in Oxford for the treatment that would enable him to unroll and read them. Chris was dying to see them. 'They might tell us what happened to the treasure but I still have an awful feeling that it was sold to help finance King Charles 1 and his war or even the family in France.'

Andrew sent off masses of film to be developed. He was also hoping to date the wood of which the beautiful table and chairs had been made. He said they could be worth a small fortune. We all tried to make sense of the conundrum and sat for ages puzzling over it. Chris thought it might be a code.

CHAPTER 16

THURSDAY

The super smells of Liz's cooking coming from the kitchen on Thursday afternoon made me wonder if cooking our own supper of baked beans and eggs in a tent was such a good idea after all. I didn't say anything though, as Guy was enjoying getting all our grub together and Liz promised to save us some chocolate pudding for afters.

At about six o'clock we struggled down to the edge of the wood with all our gear - tent, sleeping bags, a little gas stove, blankets and a ground sheet.

We carried our food in a basket - baked beans ready in a little sauce pan, a frying pan and eggs with lots of bread rolls all ready-buttered, plates and spoons and a jar of strawberry jam. It took a couple of journeys and my heel was throbbing. Then we realised that we had forgotten the mallet for bashing in the tent poles and pegs.

'Oh let's eat first.' suggested Guy. 'I'm starving. We can do the tent later.'

I soon discovered that egg, baked beans, crusty rolls with oodles of strawberry jam really do taste wonderful, especially when you've cooked it all yourself. It was a beautiful warm August evening the sun shining in a blue sky. We watched the house martins and swallows swooping up the hill and over our heads to their nests in the eves of the house. We were so full of food that we sat for ages. I had a copy of the conundrum in my pocket and we tried again, in vain, to make sense of it.

Eventually we decided to get the tent up. 'You shove all that lot into the basket,' said Guy looking at the remains of our feast. 'I'll go and get the mallet.'

We picked a spot at the edge of the wood sheltered on three sides by the trees. Guy selected one of the poles and whilst I held it still, he bashed it into the ground. 'This is a special tent. It was invented by my Great Great Grandad. He was an archaeologist as well and went digging in Egypt. The sand wouldn't hold tent pegs or poles so he had to hammer the two tent poles into the sand.'

The poles were joined by a length of cord. 'This tells us how far apart to put the poles' explained Guy. 'Right, now we'll put the other one here.' Again I held it in position but this time the pole wouldn't go into the soil. I moved it over a bit but it still would not go in more than three or four inches.

'There must be a rock down there.' I said and began picking at the soil with one of the tent pegs. 'It's a big brick!' I said as I began to drive the peg into the turf. 'It's all along here - look!' Guy by now, also armed with a tent peg, was clearing away the turf. 'Let's both work together and try to clear one spot.' I said. It would have been more sensible to move the tent altogether but by now we were determined to find out what was under there. 'We need some of those tools we used at Timothy's dig the other day.'

Finally we had cleared about a foot square of a slab of

stone. 'I think there is a carving on here. Look!' I said. 'Clear it a bit further.' Sure enough, we could make out shapes. The trouble was that the soil under the turf was wet and we couldn't clean it off. 'It's a grave stone.' said Guy 'I'm going to get somebody and I'll get some tools - we need brushes. Hope they've finished their dinner - what's the time?'

'Ten past eight.' I said.

He ran back to the house and I continued to clear the stone. He came back with a bag full of trowels and scrapers and both soft and stiff brushes. 'Uncle Chris is coming.' he said 'and Mum gave us this.' He carefully lifted out two pieces of chocolate cream gateau. We ate our cake and then continued to brush away the soil from the stone.

'Now!' said Chris as he walked towards us. 'What have you found this time?'

'It's a slab and there's a carving. It looks a bit like the family crest.' said Guy.

'You're right!' said Chris. 'Let's try and clear more of the turf away.' We set to and having lifted the grass and mud we saw the complete crest carved into a slab about two feet by three feet. 'Keep brushing. I'm going to get Andrew and Tim.'

They were back in no time at all. They all stared at the slab.

'It looks to me like a lid.' said Andrew 'But why the crest? Even to the Latin inscription.'

'Could be the cover to a well.' said Tim.

'Or a dog's grave' laughed Andrew, 'pinched from the churchyard perhaps!'

'Maybe the treasure is buried underneath.' said Guy hopefully.

Chris said he thought we would have to try to lift the stone. I was still scraping and picking away with my tent peg down one side when suddenly the point slipped down a crack and got stuck. I pulled it out and carefully pushed it back down the crack removing a mass of soil. I realised it was not a crack but a space running in a straight line along the side of the slab. I continued to clean out ages of soil from a narrow space between two stone faces. I called Chris to see what I'd found and he decided the slab must be sitting in a stone frame.

'It is a lid, I'm sure,' said Chris 'and used to cover something. Let's try to clear all round the crack.'

'It's a bit dark and gloomy now.' I said 'The sun's gone down behind the church. It's difficult to see.'

'I'm going to get some rope and a crowbar.' said Chris 'I'm sure we should be able to lift it.' He set off towards the house at a jog. Suddenly he stopped - turned - and pointed at me. He looked so fierce.

'WHAT DID YOU SAY, BOY?' He started to walk towards me.

I had to think. He looked so cross. 'This stone is sitting in a frame.' I stammered.

'No, NO! Just now - you complained you couldn't see.' He was still glaring at me.

'Oh yes! The sun has gone down behind the chapel tower; it's a bit dark and gloomy.'

He walked up to the slab, turned and looked up at the church. 'That's it!' he whispered. 'THAT'S IT! DON'T YOU SEE!' We all looked up at him puzzled.

'Er - no!' said Andrew.

'The conundrum!' he shouted. 'What's the date somebody?' 'About the 7th of August.' said Tim.

'And what's the time?' Chris looked at his watch. 'Just after 9 o'clock! What did the conundrum say? "At octo on octo of octo". That could mean a time, and perhaps a date. Don't forget that we've put the clocks on an hour, British Summer Time. It's only 8 o'clock by the sun.' I fished my copy of the conundrum out of my pocket and passed it to Chris.

'Yes,' he continued, 'At octo on octo of octo. Octo is eight in Latin. Perhaps this is 8 o'clock on the 8th day of the 8th month - which is August -YES!! Now, this line AND TALL SHADOWS GLOOM THE MIRE, see - the sun has gone down behind the chapel tower at about nine o'clock.'

'What's the mire?" I asked.

'An old English word for mud.' explained Tim.

'And look!' said Guy quietly, 'The swallows and house martins have all gone; there were masses of them flying around here earlier. What's that line?'

'OR WHEN SWALLOWS CEASE THEIR DANCE.' muttered Chris, 'Yes, yes. It's all coming together.'

'I'll bet that church tower shadow exactly covers this stone at eight o'clock on the eighth of August.' said Andrew. 'Bit scary when you remember that this conundrum was written three hundred years ago. We're a couple of days adrift of course and it's past nine o'clock but this slab is what we were supposed to find and would have done so if we'd cracked the code.'

'But how does the rest of the poem help?' I asked.

'I don't know yet.' said Chris 'But I think we must lift this slab. I'll go and get the rope and crowbar.'

We all looked at the slab. Tim and Andrew began trying to work out where the shadow would have fallen if we'd got all the numbers right.

'Run the trowels round the edges.' said Tim. 'We might be able to loosen it a bit.'

Chris arrived back and he and Andrew tried to get the crowbars under the edge at one end but the slab would not budge. We all sat around wondering what to do next.

'I've got an idea.' said Chris. 'The best thing to do is stop for today. It's getting too dark and gloomy and I think there will be a few hours work shifting this stone. Let's start tomorrow morning at 9 o'clock.

Liz, Sue, Ann and Mac all came wandering across the grass. 'It's OK.' said Liz. 'You can all come back now. We've finished the washing up! Found a grave stone indeed!' Everybody laughed. 'That's the best washing up excuse I've ever heard!'

'But we did. Look!' said Guy.

'Oh I say! Well! Whatever is it?'

'It's got the crest carved into it.' said Sue.

'We don't know,' said Chris. 'but we can't shift it. We're packing up for tonight and we'll try again in the morning.'

And so we all trooped back to the house. Guy and I didn't get our night in the tent but with all the excitement it didn't seem to matter.

CHAPTER 17

BENEATH THE STONE

I woke early next morning, my watch said twenty past six and suddenly last night's adventures came flooding back. Through my open window there was a blue sky - the sun was shining - thank goodness. As I turned over I realised there was a face peering through the open door.

'Oh good! You're awake.' said Guy. 'Let's go down to the slab now and have a go at cleaning it up - or something. I'm just dying to have another look at it.'

I was too, so we crept out of the house and hurried across the grass to our find. Imagine our surprise when we found Uncle Christopher there already.

'Good morning!' he greeted us. 'I see you're still limping, Luke. Guess you couldn't sleep either. Well come on! Don't waste time. You, Guy, get brushing and you, Luke continue cleaning out the crack along this end. We must try to get our crowbars in there. Timothy is bringing some chocks of wood which we can hopefully shove under the slab as we lift it, if we ever do; if the worst comes to the worst we may have to smash it.'

I began scraping along the groove when I realised that there was some thing very hard wedged in the crack along the end. It felt like stones jammed down. I tried to prise them out but they wouldn't budge. The slab was a dark grey slate colour but these lumps were darker. We hadn't seen them last night. I showed them to Chris and having brushed them clean with a wire brush, he got very excited.

'No wonder we couldn't get the crowbars under here last night.' he laughed. 'You've found three hinges. Look!' He pointed. 'One, two, three. We should have tried lifting the other end.'

Sure enough. The dark lumps were big metal hinges biting into the slab.

'Won't they be rusty?' asked Guy.

'Very likely!' Chris replied. 'We must be very careful. We don't want that lid crashing in on whatever is underneath.' We continued brushing and scraping the soil of ages out of the grooves.

At about 8.30am Andrew arrived followed shortly by Timothy carrying a bag of wooden chocks plus a couple of wooden mallets and a number of 4x4 lengths of wood.

They were thrilled with the 'hinges'.

'Perhaps a drop of oil might be a good idea!' somebody said. 'Go and get the oil can from the shed, please Guy. Pity we didn't see them last night. We could have soaked them in oil over-night.'

'I wonder if there is anything at the other end - perhaps a clip to keep it closed.' Andrew wandered over but after running his trowel along the groove he found nothing.

By now it was well after nine. Guy said he was starving so they decided to leave the oil soaking into the hinges for about an hour whilst we all went back to the house for coffee and breakfast.

We explained to Liz how we had found the hinges at one edge of the slab, as she served the coffee.

'Oh blow!' she said. 'Sue and I are going to Oxford today – I'm afraid we're going to miss all the fun if you get that slab open.'

. . . .

'OK. Now!' said Chris taking charge as we all stood round the slab. 'You Guy and Luke, grab yourselves a wooden chock and if we managed to lift it even a tiny bit, shove the narrow end of the wood underneath the slab.'

Andrew and Tim tried for ages to get the crowbars underneath the edge. They finally decided to chip a bit out of the stone frame as there wasn't enough room to get the crowbars into the groove.

Suddenly Tim's crowbar slipped under the slab. The other side needed a bit of help with a mallet.

They both sat on the grass grinning. 'Done it!' said Tim.

'Yes!' answered Andrew. 'Now all we need to do is open it!'

They chipped a bit more of the frame away to make room for the chocks that Guy and I held ready. Chris held a length of rope.

'Right! Everybody ready?' said Andrew. 'On three. OK, one - two - three!'

They pushed with all their weight down onto the crowbars. The slab lifted just a fraction. We all cheered.

'I don't think it's too heavy.' said Tim getting his breath back. 'It was stuck fast with three hundred years of mire - try again.'

They did and this time we managed to get a couple of chocks under the slab. The men then went along the edge hammering in the bigger chocks until there was room to wedge in one of the lengths of 4x4 to prop it open. Then taking hold of the sides and, on Andrew's one two three, pushed and pulled it up and back 'til it stood almost upright on its hinges.

'Help me lash it to that nearest tree' said Chris fastening his length of rope round the slab. 'and shove in a bigger length of wood to prop it open.'

The lid, for that's what it was, had been covering a hole - a very dark hole. We couldn't see the bottom.

'I think it's a well.' said Chris. 'But we need some more light. I'll go and get some lamps.'

It was very exciting! Chris returned and lighting up the hole, we could see a floor almost ten feet below which disappeared into a passage.

'Hold my feet.' said Chris lying on the ground leaning over into the hole. Holding the lamp at arms length down into the darkness he said 'There is a passage but it disappears. It's too dark to see. We need to get down there but we'll need the big ladder.'

'We'll get it!' said Guy setting off at a run with me hobbling after him. Reaching the house he rushed into the back door to the kitchen.

'We've found another secret passage, Mum, but we need a ladder.' He said. But there was no answer. 'She's gone to Oxford.'

We ran on to the shed, collected a long ladder and between us, hurried it back to the hole. We didn't speak, both breathless but so excited.

Meanwhile the men had lit another lamp and after placing the ladder in the hole we all carefully climbed down onto the stone floor. The walls, green with age, were built of brick. This tunnel had been dug out and the walls lined with the bricks.

'And look!' said Andrew. 'There are rusty broken brackets on this end wall, the remains of a ladder, perhaps.'

'Careful you don't slip!' said Chris.

'I wonder where it goes?' Guy whispered as we all crept along.

We stopped at a door in the wall on our left made of heavy dark wood studded with big metal headed nails.

'I'm almost afraid to open this.' said Chris.

It was fastened with a simple latch. Chris went first. The door jammed on the floor. It needed lifting and pushing to get it open.

'Been hanging too long.' muttered Tim.

We finally managed to open it and Chris went in carrying his lamp. It was a room about 10 feet almost square I think. It had a very low ceiling and the walls were of whitewashed brick. We all fanned out just inside the door not wanting to disturb anything. It had evidently been used as living quarters for a group of people. We could only guess who and when.

There were four narrow beds along one wall about the size of our camp beds but shorter. Also, two tiny little beds and a baby's wooden rocking cradle. Each had a pillow and a woollen rug.

'Oh Lordie, Lordie!' said Chris. 'You realise – all of you – this is where Harry de Ville with his wife, servants, two children and a baby lived, waiting, hiding from Oliver Cromwell, in 1649. How many days did they fearfully hide here, I wonder?'

He wandered over to the baby's cradle and gave it a gentle push, setting it rocking. Nobody said a word, all thinking about that poor terrified family.

There was a table against the opposite wall with two hard wooden chairs with high backs; three wooden stools were scattered around the little room. Shelves fastened high on the walls each held a candlestick. There were two more candlesticks on the table together with a small wooden box. Dinner plates, Chris said they were probably pewter, and spoons which he said were likely to be silver, lay scattered on the table as though a meal had just been finished. Over against the far wall were four big round wooden barrels. 'For water, probably.' said Andrew.

It all looked very lived in as though people had just popped out. There were even dents in the pillows where a head had rested and the beds were untidy as though they had just been slept in. One plate and spoon had been left lying on a bed. Someone had sat there to eat his or her meal. It was quite sad, like looking at a picture in a book. I felt we shouldn't be there and that somebody would come back in a minute and ask us who we were and what we were doing in there. There was also a strange feeling that someone was standing behind me watching. I think we all felt the same. It was all so still and quiet. Chris spoke, breaking the silence.

'Alas, how many hours and years have pass'd
Since human forms have round this table sate,
Or lamp, or taper, on its surface gleamed!'

We all looked at him; he grinned at us. 'That is a bit of poetry used by Sir Walter Scott in Ivanhoe. It was written by somebody called Orra. I learned it as a boy and it just seems to fit this sad empty room.'

'Four adult's and two children's beds plus a cradle.' whispered Andrew. 'This is where they were living, hiding, perhaps for days until the heat was off when they could make their escape out of that trap door, down the hill to the river. A friend perhaps waiting with a boat to get them safely to France.'

'Pity that they all died of plague.' I said.

'Not all.' remarked Chris. 'The baby Edward survived if you remember and was brought up by an aunt and uncle. When King Charles I's son, Charles ll, came back to his throne in England about 12 years later, Edward was then about 13. He got his father's house and lands, here, returned to him because of his father's loyalty. He lived a long life and continued the de Ville's line. But, obviously he knew nothing of this secret place or how they escaped or what his father did with the treasure. The six people who did know were all dead. I have always said they probably sold it when they needed money but since finding the conundrum, I'm not so sure. The line "Here weapons in lasting peace will lie." bothers me. Where is - HERE?'

Andrew and Tim had wandered out of the room down the passage with one of the lamps.

'I say Chris!' shouted Tim. 'Come here, look at this!'

We hurried out to find them fighting with another door at what seemed to be the end of the passage.

'Can't budge it. Expect it's probably locked but it will have dropped over the ages like the other one.'

'Perhaps there is a key in the box on that table in the room.' suggested Guy.

Andrew patted him on the head. 'Good thinking!' he said.

He went to look and came back carrying two keys on a big metal ring. One fitted the door.

To cut a long story short we pushed and lifted and pushed finally getting the door open into another whitewashed room smaller than the last and this time containing only a couple of trunks.

However, when the lamp was held high it illuminated the strangest thing of all. In the far corner there was a flight of stone steps built against the brick wall, almost reaching the ceiling but stopping about a foot short.

'I wonder where those go.' said Guy.

'Perhaps this was some sort of cellar long ago.' said Tim.

The trunks looked big and heavy. One was made of wood covered with leather and bound with metal straps. It had a domed top and was fastened at the front by a hasp held locked by a long metal nail.

The hinges creaked as the lid was opened. Lying on the top was a mass of black velvet. We carefully lifted it out. It was a cloak beautifully lined with silk with a broach-like clip at the neck. Underneath was a pair of knee length red velvet breeches and a matching jacket coat with a lace collar. There was a yellowish white cotton shirt lying neatly folded underneath.   Chris carefully lifted these clothes out. 'These must have been the Harry's.' he said.

He continued to unpack the trunk passing the items to each of us in turn to hold. Next there was a woman's dress of dark blue satin with huge sleeves and a deep lace cape around the shoulders. Then came a little girl's dress in yellow - a miniature copy of her mother's. And lastly a small boy's suit of breeches and jacket, a small shirt and a cloak exactly like his father's. There was nothing else. We had all hoped for that elusive treasure!

'Oh well.' said Chris as we replaced all the clothes. 'Let's try the other one.' And turning to the other wooden box found it locked. Andrew tried the other key on the ring. 'I think it fits!' he said and turning it with some difficulty there was a 'click' - it was open!

'Hang on a minute.' Chris looked at us all in turn. 'We must ask why would they lock this one and not the other and why would they cover that slab of stone with a ton of soil?'

'Perhaps this is where they left all their valuables.' said Guy, 'Couldn't carry them.'

'Exactly! Here are their rich expensive clothes. They'd probably escaped dressed as servants. Everything else had to be left behind. Now, if there is a treasure here in this box, I think everybody should be here when we open it. Aunt Sue, your Dad and Mum Guy, even Ann and Mac.'

'But Dad's in London!' said Guy.

'Yes,' said Chris looking at his watch. 'it's almost 12 o'clock. If we can get hold of him he might get that fast train that leaves Paddington at one-forty. He could be in Reading by two-fifty. Come on. We'll all go and get some lunch and gather everyone together later.'

Back at the house, they rang Guy's Dad but he was lecturing and would have to take a later train getting him to Reading about four.

'Best we can do.' said Chris.

Tim went home for lunch promising to meet the train at Reading. Chris and Andrew also went home for their lunch agreeing to be back later. Guy and I found some rolls and cheese. We explained to Liz, when she came home later, what we had found and that we were all to meet when Guy's Dad came home about 4 o'clock.

'I knew we'd miss all the excitement.' she laughed.

That afternoon was the longest I can remember. We couldn't wait, yet couldn't settle to do anything that would pass the time quickly. Finally at 4 o'clock, we sat on the hillside watching the road below for a sight of Tim's car.

Suddenly - there it was - that distinctive green Landrover snaking its way along the road in the distance. We rushed to the drive behind the house.

CHAPTER 18

THE TRUNK

Guy's Dad, Tim and Ann, climbed out of the Landrover accompanied by their three spaniels, Amy, Panny and Fred. Guy was jumping up and down muttering, 'Great - great - great, at last, thought you'd never get here.'

'Sorry you've had to wait.' said his Dad lifting out his bags and handing one to both Guy and me. 'Couldn't get away - so - tell me, what have you boys found this time.'

'Oh Dad! You should see it all, there's this room underground with beds, plates, chairs and tables - and there's this trunk full of clothes - and, oh I don't know where to start, there's so much down there. You have to see it all.'

'Ok! Ok! Give me time to change. I can't go down there in the only decent suit I possess. But believe me, Son, I'm dying to see it all.'

And so it was that 5 o'clock saw us all walking across the grass from the house, the four men in front, their four wives chatting together next and Guy and me bringing up the rear with the dogs.

'Why do they call Andrew's wife Mac?' I asked.

'Because her name was Mackenzie before she was

married. Andrew met her when he was on a dig in the north of Scotland. Her Christian names are Karoleen Violet but she has always been known as Mac.' Guy explained.

We all (except the dogs) climbed down the ladder into the passage. Tim masterminded the ladder and helped the ladies over the edge of the hole and onto the first rungs. The sun had been hot on our backs as we had walked across but now the dark passage felt quite cold.

'We should have put on a sweater.' said Sue. 'I should think it was cold living down here.'

Chris and Andrew went ahead with a lamp each. We all followed into the first room and stood once again just inside the door. One of the ladies said 'Oh my goodness!'

'I know what it reminds me of.' whispered Tim. 'One of those rooms they set up in museums to show how people lived and worked in days gone by.'

'Yes, but this room is real - we're just short of the people!' answered Ann 'And it feels as though they have just popped out.'

'It's a bit creepy I must say.' said Mac.

Tim and Andrew set up their lights for the photographs that they needed for the records.

'Don't forget to get that plate and spoon on the bed.' said Guy.

'Let's leave them to their photography.' said Chris. 'Come, ladies, we'll show you the fabulous collection of 17th century costume.'

We all trooped after Chris including Guy's Dad. The beautiful clothes were once again taken out of the trunk much to the ladies' delight, especially the gown belonging to the wife.

'Gosh, she was so small!' said Sue 'I'm only 5ft 1" and she was much smaller than that.'

'Look!' said Mac 'The bodice is embroidered with tiny pearls - it's so lovely. I bet she hated leaving this behind.'

'Probably,' answered Chris 'But don't forget they had intended to come back one day and talking about leaving things behind let's find out what was left behind in this other trunk which is the reason we got everybody together. Go and get the others, Guy, and let's get it open.'

Andrew held the lamp high over the trunk.

'*You* must open it.' said Chris looking at Aunt Sue and her brother. Guy's Dad looked at his sister and they walked to opposite ends of the box and both taking hold of the lid, lifted it open.

Nobody spoke.

Lying on the top of a stretch of linen was what Chris said later was a page of parchment on which was written a few sentences followed by a list.

'Bring the lamp a little nearer, please.' said Chris as he lifted out the parchment and slowly began to read: -

'In these troubled times may God protect us all and may he protect and keep the soul of our Dearest King Charles, cruelly murdered by the present rulers of our land.'

'Within, I leave my wealth in safety to await my return in happier times.'

'And here' said Chris holding up the parchment for us all to see 'is the list of what is in the box. You'll have to bear with me. It's written in the old English of their times and it is not easy to read. Crusader's sword. Golden scimitar and scabbard. Salt. Two silver stirrups. Gold altar plate. Two gold candlesticks. One gold crucifix. Twelve gold table trenchers. Twelve silver forks. Twelve silver spoons. Twelve apostle spoons. Two pearl necklaces. Ten finger rings. Ruby necklace. Diamond necklace. Diamond and emerald headdress. Gold chain. Six pairs silver shoe buckles. Sword belt and sword. Two pairs pistols. One gold and jeweled altar chalice. Coin.'

'Is this the treasure, Mum?' whispered Guy.

'I think so.' she replied putting an arm round his shoulders.

The room was very quiet. No one spoke.

'Very difficult to read!' muttered Chris. 'Fs and Ss all mixed up. Well - ' he looked at everyone standing round the box. 'shall we unpack it?'

Aunt Sue and Guy's Dad looked at each other and both said 'Yes!' together.

'OK - here goes - gosh I'm shaking!' said Chris. 'I'm not sure whether it's excitement or fear!'

'Bit of both I suggest!' said Sue 'Not knowing what we're going to find, but all hoping it's the lost treasure.'

The large piece of linen cloth was tucked on top neatly covering whatever was underneath. Chris removed it and passed it to Ann who carefully folded it. Underneath were what seemed to be several different shaped parcels all carefully wrapped in linen cloths. Everyone looked at each other. All seemed afraid to touch the contents. Lying on top was quite a big parcel.

'Gosh this is heavy!' muttered Chris lifting it out and,

removing the linen, found a solid gold cross. 'This is from the altar in the chapel, I guess.' he said. It stood on a square marble base and was about two feet high. 'Put it over there on those steps, Guy.' said Chris.

Nestling next to where the crucifix had been was a smaller bundle. Chris lifted it out and after running his hands over it he looked around at us all and said quietly 'I think I know what this is!' I think we were all holding our breath as it was unwrapped and we all gasped at the sight lying in Chris' hands. It was the scimitar locked safely in its scabbard.

'What a beautiful thing!' someone said and it surely was. The scimitar and its scabbard were made of solid gold the whole thing being about a foot long. The scabbard was encrusted with jewels of red and green all set in frames of hundreds of pearls. The grip of the scimitar was also set with jewels. 'Two big diamonds, rubies and sapphires!' Timothy said.

Then Chris carefully pulled the scimitar out of the scabbard. It shone like a mirror in the light of the lamps. 'Looks as though it was made last week!' said Guy's Dad taking it from Chris. 'There's not the slightest mark or scratch on it - - - - magnificent!'

Everyone was very quiet. Each of us held it in turn. Guy's Dad looked at Liz. 'Priceless!' he said 'Priceless!' She, holding the scabbard, nodded and said 'It's nearly nine hundred years old! I can't believe it. It's beautiful. These pearls, simply hundreds of them, all graduated, different sizes into these swirling patterns around the gems.' She handed it back and we watched as Chris replaced the scimitar and re-wrapped it. 'What are the gems, I wonder?' he said.

'Probably rubies, emeralds and diamonds.' replied Tim. 'But we can't be sure yet.'

Next out was a sword. 'This I think may be the original sword which came back with Guy from Damascus.' said Chris. 'The sword on the family crest!'

'The one Davoud used as a crutch when he couldn't walk!' said Guy taking it off Chris. 'And I am here, now, holding it!'

'Yes!' smiled Chris. 'There's another one here too. Much later. Probably from the 1600s and maybe belonging to Harry himself. I'm surprised he didn't take it with him although if he was travelling as a peasant he wouldn't want to be found carrying such a fine expensive weapon. He had already given Daniel his father's sword, the records tell us.'

Next was what was called a Salt. Chris explained that it was a very valuable piece of tableware made to hold the salt. Salt crystals in those days were a precious commodity. Our Salt was made of gold encrusted with emeralds. 'This is said to have been a gift to the family by Queen Elizabeth 1 in 1575 after a visit.'

'Put all these things over there on the steps' said Chris 'until we get the box emptied.' And we did.

Slowly the box was unpacked of all the precious things. Guy and I carried them over one by one and carefully laid them on the flight of strange stone and brick steps which seemed to go nowhere except to the ceiling. There was some beautiful jewelry, both ladies' and men's. A solid gold chain, obviously worn by Harry, was long and very heavy. Tim put it on and joked that it was heavy enough to break his neck.

And so the treasures continued to be slowly unpacked, silver buckles for shoes, silver spoons, and strange two pronged forks, twelve gold dinner plates, a fine gold tiara studded with diamonds and rubies together with a matching necklace both nestling in a beautiful velvet lined silver box.

Chris, coming to the bottom of the box, said 'I think that's it!' and leaning into the box lifted a large piece of woolen cloth that he thought was the lining of the bottom.

'Oh my giddy aunt!' he said. Everybody peered into the box - lying neatly packed all over the bottom were small draw stringed leather pouches. Chris lifted one out and opened the top. It was full of gold coins and on closer inspection, he realised that every little bag was full of silver or gold coins.'

'There must be hundreds of thousands of pounds in value here alone ,' said Guy's Dad. 'not counting that lot on the steps!'

Guy and I sat on the floor beside the steps waiting for somebody to say something but nobody did.

'I'll tell you something, Dad.' whispered Guy.

'What's that?'

'You'll be able to afford to fix the roof and that cracked wall in the west wing.'

'Yes, Son, we will.'

Aunt Sue was crying into a big handkerchief she had pinched from Chris. 'I can't believe it.' she said. 'All this lying here for centuries - and we found it - all because you boys couldn't drive a tent pole into the ground!' She grinned at us through her tears.

'I think we'd better wrap it all up again and pack

it back into the box. We'll have to get it up into the house somehow,' said Andrew. 'for photography and cataloguing but I fear the bottom will fall out of that box if we try to lift it.'

'I've just had a thought.' remarked Tim. 'Is it treasure trove I wonder?'

'I don't know.' said Chris. 'But you two' he looked at Sue and Guy's Dad 'can trace your ancestry back to Charles I and even back to 1066 with records to prove who you are.'

'Let's not worry about that just now.' said Guy's Dad. 'Let's just enjoy looking at and handling these wonderful treasures which have been lying here under our feet for three hundred years. I still can't believe it. I'm half expecting to wake up in a minute and find myself in my bed. Do you remember, Sue,' he said, looking at his sister 'as children we used to pretend that we had found the sword and the scimitar? In those days of course we didn't know that other treasures were involved. The first information we had about these was in the list found in the box that fell out of the chimney.'

Aunt Sue came over to the stone steps where Guy and I were sitting and where everything from the box was neatly standing on the flight above us. She picked up one of the boxes. It contained the diamond necklace. 'This is exquisite' she said. 'and as your Dad said - priceless.'

And then it happened! With a slight splutter and a gurgle the hurricane lamp went out. There was absolute silence. We were plunged into darkness. Then somebody, I think it was Tim, sang 'And then the lights went out! Deedah deedah! Deedah deedee!'

'This is where in films the baddies rush in - steal the treasure - and vanish.' said Guy's Dad. Everybody laughed. 'Where is the other lamp?'

'In the other room.' somebody said. 'I'll go and get it. Can't see a thing though. Anybody got some matches?'

Andrew flicked his cigarette lighter. The flame lit up the room. 'Take this.' he said. Tim took it and set off down the long passage leaving us once again in total darkness.

'Everybody stay quite still. We don't want to stand on or break anything.' said Guy's Dad.

In the black dark, sitting by the stone steps, I was suddenly aware of a white patch on my hand. I touched it with my other hand but then it was on that hand. Then I moved my hand and the patch was on my knee. Moving my hand from side to side I realised it was a beam of bright light coming from somewhere in the ceiling over my head. In the total darkness it was a very bright thin needle of light.

'Look at this!' I said to nobody in particular.

'Look at what?' Chris chuckled. 'Can't see a thing in here at this moment, boy, total blackout!'

'No. Look over here - at me - at this. What is it? It's like daylight coming from the ceiling.'

'Good heavens!' said Chris 'You're right. It is a beam of light.'

'It looks like a tiny hole in the roof.' said Andrew.

Just then we could hear Tim coming down the passage shouting 'New lamps for old! Wooooooargh!'

'Must be Aladdin!' said his wife.

'No!' said Tim 'I am the genie of the lamp!' Everybody

giggled but was glad of the light. I was certainly a bit scared in the darkness.

'Let's get all this packed away in the box.' said Chris. 'Then we can investigate your daylight, Luke!'

'Daylight! What daylight?' asked Tim.

'Over here! But it's not so easy to see now the lamp light is back.'

We packed everything back into the trunk and then Andrew turned the lamp down low. There, sure enough, was the beam of light coming from the corner of the ceiling above the steps.

I suddenly noticed that there were bits of grit and stone on the steps. I picked a bit up. 'Look at this.' I said.

They turned up the lamp and Guy's Dad picked up the bits of grit and rubbed it between his fingers. 'It's plaster! See!' and picking up another bit he crumbled it to powder.

'Oh dear.' whispered Guy. 'I think I hit the roof with the tip of that sword.'

'Yes, and you've chipped away a bit of the ceiling in the corner - anybody got a penknife?' Andrew had and handed it to Guy's Dad. 'I'll chip a bit more off and see what's underneath.' He started chipping away at the tiny hole running the blade along the edge and soon quite a bit of light seemed to be coming in along the crack against the wall. 'I seem to be pulling the ceiling down.'

Andrew and Tim scrambled up the steps and helped breaking up the plaster and chipping it away. Soon it was falling down in lumps and creating such a dust. They were covered by the white powder.

'What is it?' asked Guy.

'It's ancient plaster.' said Andrew. 'It was used to cover the rough bricks much as we do today but they made it in those days from lime, horsehair, perhaps fine straw or chaff and a good dollop of wet mud all mixed together like a pudding. Then they slapped it on the walls and when it was dry gave it a coat of white lime which acted like paint. Somebody has slapped this on here. All the ceiling is covered with it as you see but this corner is different. As we chip it away I'm beginning to think that this plaster is covering, even hiding something.'

'Look at this!' said Tim. 'I've uncovered a metal clip.'

As they continued to tear away the plaster a square lid started to appear.

'I think it's a trap door.' said Chris who had patiently held the hurricane lamp for the others and who was now covered in white dust and lumps of plaster.

'A trap door to - where? Asked Sue. 'We're too far from the house.'

'I've been puzzling over this. We really are fools. I know exactly where we are.' Everyone looked at Chris and he grinned, glancing from one face to the other in the lamp light. 'We're right under the chapel!'

'Of course!' said Guy's Dad.

'They vanished from the chapel!' whispered Guy in my ear. 'And they came down here.'

By now all the plaster from the square section in the corner over the steps had been cleared. It was obviously a trap door. Two large clips attached to its sides appeared to fasten it to the ceiling holding it down in place. There was a flat handle embedded in the middle which had been covered by the plaster.

'Seems to me that it's a kind of lid over this square hole.' said Guy's Dad.

'Yes!' said Chris. 'But what about these clips?'

'Well, I think one end of each clip is set on a pivot in the lid. They will probably swing round on their pivot releasing the lid which will then push up and over.'

Having agreed that the clips were attached to the lid, they tried to push the end round but they had been clipped tight for so long that they wouldn't budge. 'We need a hammer.' said Andrew. 'Those mallets we brought to drive the chocks under the stone are in the bag in the passage.'

'I'll get them.' said Tim setting off, lighting his way with Andrew's lighter.

Andrew and Tim then took a mallet each and carefully tapped the clips sideways away from the ceiling. It was a slow job but once they started to slide sideways on their pivots they moved faster and faster. One side was released and with one final tap on the second clip it too came apart. The lid seemed to lift up from its frame a fraction of an inch.

'See!' pointed out Guy's Dad. 'To close it you pull it down and slide the clips across into place, holding it down. However we've now got to open it so let's try pushing upwards.'

That didn't work although all three men crowded onto the steps and pushed upwards with all their might.

'I've got an idea!' said Tim. 'Perhaps it moves sideways. Has anybody got a bit of paper on them?'

'I've got an envelope.' said Chris.

'That might do.' And taking it he passed it along the

fine crack that had appeared all around the square 'lid'. 'I thought so. There is a restriction at this back corner. Another pivot rod perhaps, or a spring.'

'Well now.' muttered Chris. 'Let's think. If we are going to walk up the steps and out, we face this way; and if that is a pivot under that back right-hand corner behind us, we have to push this lid sideways swinging it out to the right. That will then, hopefully, clear the hole. Push the handle back in place!'

He was right but it took a lot of pushing to move it. But bit by bit each man trying in turn pushed the lid sideways and back off the hole. At one stage the space was big enough for Guy's Dad to get his head through the gap. We heard him say 'Flipping Nora!' He came down again and sat on the steps laughing.

'WELL?' said Liz.

'Yes!' he laughed. 'We're under the chapel right enough. But you'll never guess what it is we're shoving out of the way of this hole!' We all waited.

'Well tell us, for Goodness Sake!' said Liz to her husband.

Still giggling, he looked round at all of us. 'THE FONT!'

'THE FONT!' everybody said together.

CHAPTER 19

INTO THE CHAPEL

'As soon as there is room we'll push you two slim-jim boys up and you can give us a hand by giving it a push from up there.' After much pushing and shoving, the font was slowly moved away from the hole.

'We're the first people out of this room since Harry and his family vanished.' remarked Chris as he clambered out. 'I should imagine the font was easier to move in those days. That pivot is rusted almost to breaking point and the font is now scratching the floor. Must get some grease on the pivot. Lucky it didn't give way.'

'Yes - but we've pushed it wide open.' said Andrew. 'Remember that they were small people, in a hurry to get down into that tunnel. They would have opened it just enough to squeeze through, the men pushing the children and the ladies in first, handing down the baby and finally climbing down themselves. Poor souls - they must have been shaking - terrified. Maybe they had a few rehearsals in the weeks before, Harry perhaps suspecting that Cromwell would be coming for him.'

'But I think,' said Guy's dad, 'that this secret hideaway under the chapel was created years before Harry and his family used it. Probably used it as a store for valuables or hiding people from the law.'

I was thinking about them climbing down those steps and then pulling the font back into place. 'If they had had as much trouble closing it as we had getting it open, they would have been caught for sure.' I said.

The evening sun was shining through the stained glass windows, the colours dancing on the floor as the trees broke up the shafts of sunlight. There, again, was the red blood-like stain.

'What time is it?' asked Chris. 'My watch has stopped.'

Everybody had found a seat on a pew; the men were exhausted from their efforts. We were all quiet. There seemed to be nothing to say, all lost in our own thoughts of gold, treasure and that family of so long ago. They must have been terrified sitting underneath listening to the sounds of the soldiers searching for them above in the chapel.

'It's about half past seven.' said Tim in answer to Chris' question. Chris gazed at the floor looking at the colours moving around our feet.

'That's it - isn't it?' said Chris quietly.

'What?' said Guy's Dad.

'The other bit of the conundrum. How stupid we are; we have always said that the sun's reflection through that red cloak onto the floor looks like a blood stain. But as the sunlight moves across the window and the shadow moves over the font, the red is broken up by the trees - then it looks like flames. Hence AT THE BAPTISM OF BLOOD AND FIRE. Your ancestors, Guy, had the same idea but they knew something we didn't.' He looked around at all of us sitting so quietly listening to him. 'Although the sun plays tricks with those colours most of the year round they pass over the font at about eight o'clock around the eighth of August and probably sometime in May.'

'But this is the eighth month of the year!' said Sue. 'There! Look at the rainbows moving across the floor now, from the other colours in the window! Where's that poem?' I passed her my tatty copy from my pocket and she read it.

'At octo on octo of octo - of course - at eight o'clock - on the eighth day - of the eighth month!' she continued. 'When rainbows merrily prance - there they are prancing! At the baptism of blood and fire - here, I would never have thought of the font. The word baptism threw us a bit. We tend to christen babies at the font these days. We use the words christen and christening but in those days they probably said baptise and baptism.' She continued to read the poem.

'Or when swallows cease their dance
And tall shadows gloom the mire
Here weapons in lasting peace will lie
But mark well my words You Sirs
Lest I should die'

'And of course,' added Guy's Dad. 'When SWALLOWS CEASE THEIR DANCE or flying for the night and that line TALL SHADOWS GLOOM THE MIRE when the sun goes down behind the church tower - all happens about 8.00pm. Seems so simple now.'

'That was clever.' said Guy.

'It was,' replied his Dad. 'too clever for us, although

we didn't try very hard to solve his puzzle. We should have got the bit about the rainbows but we would never have realised we had to move the font and yet, they had to go somewhere; the family didn't disappear into thin air. They didn't go up so they must have gone down. There must be a way to release those clips from up here, otherwise the only way into their secret hideout would be under the slab in the wood.'

'It must have been unclipped, ready just to slide open but what would have happened if Daniel and the soldiers had gone into the church with them I wonder?' said Guy.

'Well that would have been another story.' said Chris.

'I wonder if Harry's friend Daniel knew about the secret under the font and perhaps knew where they had gone? He might have sat on the font!' I joked

'Maybe. We'll never know.' replied Andrew.

'But their escape must have been planned weeks in advance.' said Liz. 'Food, clothing, bedding, water, all had to be in place in the secret rooms when they went into the chapel that day. Only their two faithful servants would have known about their plans and keeping them a secret would have been very difficult. We know Cromwell had paid spies in every rich Royalist household.'

'Imagine what an awful time they must have had living down there, knowing Cromwell would leave no stone unturned in his effort to find them and with a baby too. Poor people.' Ann added.

'Daniel did give Harry a couple of days warning.' pointed out Chris. 'Although Harry must have known Cromwell would come after him sometime, so I guess it was all planned weeks in advance. Somebody had to be waiting with a boat on the Thames to get them away one dark night, remember.'

'Talking about dark nights,' said Guy's Dad. 'I think we had better close up that hole over the other end of the tunnel before it gets too dark to see. Don't want anything falling in.'

'Yes,' said Chris. 'But let's close down those trunks underneath and let's just push a couple of pews over this hole. I couldn't face shoving that font back again tonight.'

'All that priceless treasure sitting down there!' whispered Guy's Dad. 'All the things we've always wanted to do with the house,' he continued looking from his sister Sue to his wife, 'not least a new roof, new tarmac for the drive, replace the thatch on your farmhouse roof, Andrew, and to be able to work perhaps part time and really get down to the excavations by the river.'

When everything was secured for the night and we had collected the dogs who were still waiting patiently by the hole in the wood we all walked back to the house. I heard the owls hooting but, oh gosh, we were all so tired.

'Have to find some easier way of swinging that font backwards and forwards.' said Andrew. 'My shoulders are killing me.'

The ladies made hot drinks. The men had beer. Guy and I had milk. We all sat round the big kitchen table discussing the day and the marvelous family treasure.

'It's funny!' said Sue looking at her brother. 'Grandfather never did find anything really exciting in all his years working in archaeology, Egypt, Mesopotamia, Turkey. And yet his funny old tent with its funny old tent pole pointed the way to probably one of the biggest treasures ever found - and it's ours!'

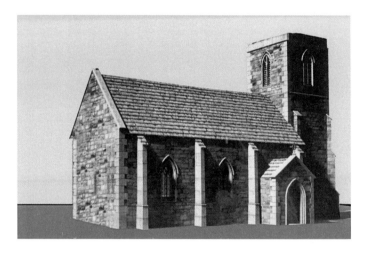

The Chapel

CHAPTER 20

THE FINISH

Next day everybody helped carry everything back into the house. We laid it all out on the big dining table. The find was reported to the authorities and serious looking men with briefcases, dark suits and collars and ties, came to look at it. Hundreds of photographs were taken. There were, by the way, 140 small bags of silver and gold coins at the bottom of the box. It represented over £2,000,000 in monetary value but was worth much more than that as many of the coins carried the head of Queen Elizabeth 1, some were minted in James 1's time and the rest from Charles 1. Most of them were gold and a few silver but nearly all were in almost mint condition.

The following week we were all on the National TV News. All the treasures were still laid out on the dining table and when lit by the powerful TV lights they looked fabulous. 'It's like Aladdin's cave!' said the TV presenter.

Guy and I had to tell them how we found the tunnel quite by accident when we tried to put up the old tent. The story of Harry and his family escaping to France, all dying of plague except the baby Edward and how the secrets of the treasure were forgotten, made a wonderful documentary. Somebody said it should be made into a film. My parents and Grandmother came to Guy's house with my now recovered Grandpa. He was laughingly thanked for having his accident in France for without it I would never have needed to go to Guy's and the treasure probably never found.

The treasure was all finally stored in the vault of a big London bank. Guy's parents gave me a very generous gift of money, which was put into a trust until I reached the age of 21, as they said that without me, the treasure would not have been found.

Guy and I both went on to study archaeology. He's in Wiltshire on a dig at the moment. I inherited my grandparent's cottage on the cliffs overlooking the Atlantic. Guy's parents still live in the manor house and Aunt Sue and Uncle Chris still live in the Lodge. Andrew, Timothy and Guy's Dad are all on the dig with Guy. I'm going to join them next week.

Guy's Dad gave both Tim and Andrew a generous gift of money too for their help in recovering the treasure and for pushing the font! Some of the items we found have been sold including some of the coins (although I do have one of each in a little display case on my wall just to remind me). The proceeds from these sales enabled the family to repair the house and cottages, to travel and also allowed Guy's Father to fund archeological digs all over the world. But best of all they never needed to sell the manor or their land for a holiday camp.

Guy and I did have other holidays in that lovely old house; I'll tell you about them another time but I think that is just about the end of this story. It has taken some three months to remember it all and put it all together. Guy was able to help at times by filling in bits I had forgotten and Christopher's own account, which was finally published, was also a great help. My wife, Georgie, helped with the editing.

Well, that's it. I hope I've left nothing out but I really must stop. I'm going to take our dogs, Floss, Regan and Bailey, for a walk; our sons, Andrew and Timothy, are coming down for the weekend and I have to collect them from Bodmin Station.

BIBLIOGRAPHY

I have taken no direct quotations from the following books except the poem by Orra, but I would like to thank their authors for a wealth of background colour and fact.

World War 2: -
    'Berlin Diary' *by William L. Shirer.*
    'Spitfire!' *by Sqn Ldr B. J. Ellan*
    'Spitfire.' *by John Vader.*

Civil War: -
    'Battles Royal' *by H. Miles Brown.*
    'Charles 1.'
    'Cavaliers and Roundheads.'
    (The English Civil War 1642 - 1649.)

Both the latter by Christopher Hibbert without whose encouragement this book would not have been written.

Crusades: -
    'Memoirs of the Crusades'
    by Villehardouin and De Joinville.
    'The First Crusade' *by Steven Runciman*
    'Lionhearts' *by Geoffrey Regan.*
    'The Crusades' *by Zoe Oldenbourg.*
    'Crusades' *by Terry Jones and Alan Ereira.*
    'Deus Lo Volt' *by Evan S. Connell.*
    'Dungeon, Fire and Sword' *by John J. Robinson.*
    'Knights Templar' *by Stephen Howarth.*
    'The Freemason's Guide to the Knights Templar in Scotland.' *(Edited by James Green)*
    'Ivanhoe' and 'Talisman' *by Sir Walter Scott.*

ABOUT THE AUTHOR

Betty Balmford was born and lived her early years in Birmingham. She left school at 14 and for the next seven years, worked packing chocolates for the famous Cadbury Bros Ltd. For the next four years she then trained and qualified as a nurse at the General Hospital Birmingham. After qualifying as a midwife in Plymouth and London, Paddington, Betty was commissioned into the Princess Mary's Royal Air Force Nursing Service.

She met her husband, David, an RAF pilot, in Singapore. She wrote and produced two pantomimes also in Singapore, on a later posting. They have two sons and between them all, ran a delicatessen in Henley-on-Thames for 16 years. Betty's last opus was a production, on the Wadebridge Townhall stage, of 'Modified Rapture', a story of Gilbert and Sullivan, with the Stage-A-Chord group. She lives in Cornwall and this is her first published book.